THE
VICTORIOUS
MINDSET

CHIP ESAJIAN'S

THE VICTORIOUS MINDSET

YOU WERE CREATED FOR EXTRAORDINARY

"UNLOCK THE COMMAND CENTER OF YOUR BRAIN AND CREATE EXTRAORDINARY HAPPINESS AND VICTORIOUS ABUNDANCE IN YOUR LIFE THAT WILL TAKE OTHERS BREATH AWAY"

THE Victoriour mindret

Published by: Donnalnk Publications, L.L.C.

Cover Design: The Mule, United Kingdom.
Editorial Team: Mrs. Lisa Esajian, Mr. James Weber, Mr. Philip Bartholomew, Mr. Quante Bryant and Ms. Dana Queen.

Published in the United States of America.
ISBN: 978-1-978-1-939425-03-4 print; ISBN: 978-1-939425-04-1 digital.
Second Edition Digital I Second Edition Print - 2014.

Copies of this book can be ordered by contacting:
Donnalnk Publications, L.L.C.
4405 S. Kirkman Rd., Orlando, FL 32811
www.donnaink.org I (888) 564-7741

Library of Congress Cataloging-in-Publication Data. 2013936105
Esajian, Chip – Author, 2014.
    The Victorious Mindset / Chip Esajian.
        318 p. cm.
        ISBN – 13 – 978-1-939425-03-4 (alk. paper)
        ISBN – 13 - 978-1-939425-04-1 (alk. digital)
            [1-Self-Help, 2-Non-Fiction, 3-Motivation, 4-Coaching, 5-Inspirational, 6-Education, 7-Young Adult, 8-Contemporary, 9-Business, 10-Personal Growth, 11-Self-Improvement, 12-Self-Esteem, 13-Health Mind Body, 14-Health & Fitness.]
Second Edition 10 9 8 7 6 5 4 3 2; August 2014.

TESTIMONIALS

"Powerful! Empowering! Beautiful! I loved reading this book from beginning to end, then going back and relishing each simple chapter. It is an easy read, you don't want to put it down, and most importantly how reading this book makes you feel. I feel unstoppable! I am grateful! I am excited! I feel I can do anything! What an amazing feeling!"
                    Yael

"As a Licensed Therapist with a Bachelor's degree, two Master's and a PhD in Clinical Psychology; plus over 25 years' experience working in the mental health profession, I was extremely impressed with Chip's book, "The Victorious Mindset". Having read literally hundreds of Spiritual/Self-Help books throughout my career, I was especially excited about how pragmatic and simple his program is outlined in the book. It blew my mind that without a formal education in psychology, Chip was able to accurately identify the process of positive cognitive, behavioral and emotional change. As a proponent of bibliotherapy, "The Victorious Mindset" will definitely be one of the books I suggest to my clientele in my private practice."
                    Dr. Richie Cole
                    Director
                    DRAT Therapeutiks

"I'm privileged and grateful to have had the opportunity to read Chip's book. It is touching,

heartfelt, inspirational and uplifting. It's a testament to the individual Chip has become through his experiences. 'The Victorious Mindset' will transform so many lives for the better! A must read!"

Joy Bing Fleming MBA, CC
Certified Life and Career Coach,
LifePassion.net

"The quicker you forgive the quicker you can REALLY begin to live" was really the turning point for me after reading 'The Victorious Mindset.' This book has helped me to identify and target my role in this wonderful journey of becoming the person I have only dreamed I could be in this beautiful opportunity we call life. This book is a 'MUST' read for everyone who is ready to go down a 'different road' to the next step in becoming everything 'extraordinary' that you have always wanted to become. Join us, be brave and take control of your Mindset today!"

Lisa Beavers
Intervention, Treatment and Recovery
Counselor

"Extraordinary, Motivational, Inspirational and Caring are just a few words that describe Chip Esajian . . . his message is powerful and uplifting, pay attention to his words of wisdom for they are life changing!"

Chadi Bazzi
Business Architect

"I have a saying that I live my life by ... 'Strategy Matters and Passion Rules!' I speak and work with thousands of people and Chip Esajian is one of the people who exemplify this saying to the highest degree! His message in this book (and his mission in life) is

100% uplifting. This is a book you need to be reading right now!"
Tom Ferry, New York Times Best
Selling Author of, Life! By Design

"This book will revolutionize your life! I have known Chip for over 20 years and I have personally watched his life transform in front of my eyes. From ashes to oil he has renewed his mind and become a powerful, positive force in this world. I rank this book a #1 must read to make this year the most prosperous and dynamic year ever!"
Dr. Phil Aguilar
Doctor of Divinity

"Chip is a Powerful, Dynamic, "on-fire-for-life" guy, whose calling is to help you go from ordinary to 'Extraordinary!' This book will literally change the way you look at life and your circumstances!

Chip's zeal and excitement for others encourages me to keep my focus on the ABUNDANCE mindset so I can be 'full on' for others. 'The Victorious Mindset' is a simple system to powerfully change your life!"
Tina Herz
Internet Marketer, tinaherz.com

"I absolutely loved this book. It is easy to read, follow and absorb. The references to everyday life make it more realistic. This book has inspired me to continue to move on with my life creating extraordinary! I have already picked it up a second time to practice the victorious quotes. Any age could and will benefit from the valuable information in this book. You just need to know how to read and follow instructions. Your book has made a huge impact on my life during all the

transitions I have been making and I am making them all extraordinary with my victorious mindset you have inspired!"

D'Ann L. Jacobs
RN, BSN, LNC

"Reading the Victorious Mindset has been an empowering experience. It is easy to read and clearly written. It gives a new approach to 'self-help' and engages you to look at yourself. It motivates you to wanna be a better person. I am so excited to begin the worksheets and start on healing my life. Kudos to Chip for taking his life experiences to help others find peace and contentment with theirs. This is extraordinary work!"

Rosanne Maestas-Olds
Wellness Coach

"Reading 'The Victorious Mindset' was extraordinary to say the least! Without realizing it, Chip has taken the basic tenets of cognitive behavioral therapy and proven them to be correct. He has shown, through his own experience, that people can indeed change their thoughts, which in turn can change their emotions and their behaviors. He puts what could be years of therapy in an easy to read format which anyone can follow. I would highly recommend this book to friends and clients alike!"

Carol McCormack
MSW

"When I first read the book, I knew I had to do the steps. This is the single most encouraging life transformation book I have read! Its easy to follow steps are a promising vision of a life that was once unimaginable; the work will make you a stronger empowered version

of yourself. Great job Chip! I'm looking forward to your follow up. You are truly an inspiration to all."
Melody Neary FMLP
DV/SA.C.I.C

"I personally witnessed Chip Transform his mindset and his life in a matter of just a few weeks with the thoughts principals and ideas he shares in this book. These are not just theories, they are practical and they are powerful!"
Tom Pelton, Manager
Prudential Calif. Realty

"I have spent many years training in the human development arena of Spirituality, Structural Design and Financial Education. Furthermore, I have been a world martial arts champion, designer and builder of the 10 million dollar Bat mobile, and have spent many years in the study and practice as an investment banker. I have studied a wide variety of books and known many teachers in the self-help field. Chip Esajian's book, 'The Victorious Mindset,' ranks at the very top of my long list of books and teachers. Chip Esajian conveys limitless energy and power inspiration, which will power jumpstart you toward a path of victory and fulfillment in your life!"
Steve Sakane
Leader of Security and Peace of Mind

Once we began to read this book, we weren't able to put it down. Extraordinary Powerful Book! If others apply these simple steps to their lives each day, they will notice changes in their thoughts and lives right away! We know it will empower anyone of us who is willing to admit "It's time to change what I am doing"! This book says it all, if you wish to change your life, its right here

in Chip's book, on how to do just that. It has been an honor to read "The Victorious Mindset"!
> Joseph Stricklin and Pamala Taylor Stricklin

"make no moment ordinary for every moment is EXTRAORDINARY."

CHIP ESAJIAN

MOTIVATIONAL COACH

CONTENTS

PREFACE

Happiness Victory Extraordinary Prosperity

Peace   Joy   Abundance

Stop for a moment, and consider the 7 words listed above in relation to you. Take notice of what your mind is saying to you about those words. What does your body feel when you read those 7 words? Could be, you've experienced and felt some of them, or all of them. They represent good feelings, right? Good experiences, right? Or perhaps you don't really care; maybe you haven't had a whole lot of good things happen to you in life. Maybe those words above and other words like them kind of bother you or get under your skin.

Stay with me here a little bit longer. Also, hold on to the feelings and thoughts you have about those 7 words a little bit longer too, as I ask you about chocolate. Yes chocolate. If you're like me and really love chocolate, how would you describe the taste of chocolate to someone else who has never tasted it? And, for those 17 people out there in the world, who don't like chocolate, go ahead and pick one of your favorite food items for this example.

Now, you could probably do a pretty good job of describing the taste, texture, and flavor of chocolate; but would that person end up really knowing what chocolate tasted like from your description? Most likely not. You and I both know that they would just have to taste it themselves to know for sure. And as soon as they did, they would have an "AHA" moment; which is a moment of sudden realization and insight, of how good it tastes. They would have feelings of excitement and enjoyment; and I want to do that for you, the reader, right here, with my book.

I want you to have lots of "AHA" moments in life. Whether you are living a life right now of barely surviving, feeling down, thinking you'll never get to experience what you want out of life. Or, if you're on the other end of the scale in life and you have it all, but you want more. Then there are the majority of you who are somewhere in between the 'all' or 'nothing'. Well then hang with me here a little bit longer and let's work on this 'box of chocolates' together. This will be a fun journey!

The Victorious Mindset is where I want to take you. Yes, the word "victory" is one of those *7 words* previously mentioned, and as hard as I tried in life, I just could not seem to experience "victory" often enough. When I did experience it, I seemed unable to maintain that wonderful feeling for very long. Victory at work . . . fail. Victory in relationships . . . fail. Victory with finances . . . fail. Let's try some of the others. Joy at work . . . fail. Peace of mind... fail. You get what I'm saying, right? I thought I must be doing something wrong. Perhaps I was missing a step, or just unlucky. I tried to fill in the holes in my life with money, vacations, work, fun stuff, expensive 'toys', food, alcohol, and other people. Nothing satisfied me for very long. I just wanted to be happy all the time, but I just could not maintain it. It seemed too hard to maintain happiness in anything because it was always followed by failure or disappointment. I felt like there had to be more to it. I got real curious and started asking myself some questions that seemed too big to answer. What was I doing in life? Why can't things just work out right? What's my purpose in life? What was I meant to do?"

From there, I decided I would figure out how to just be happy, all the time, regardless of what was happening in my life. Regardless of my finances, my job, where I lived, what I owned or didn't own, how I dressed, etc. I figured out that, everything I thought about came from what I believed in. I figured out I could change my life by changing my beliefs. You see, what you believe, in your mind, turns into a thought, and that thought turns into an attitude, the attitude becomes an emotion, emotion to a behavior, into words and finally into actions – which are all controlled by what you believe in, your belief system, your mindset.

The Victorious Mindset is a training system of personal empowerment over your life. A simple, 10-step system to teach you how to create the life you want. Whether you know what you want or not, it all starts with you being able to create a Victorious Mindset. It is important for you to know that you can accomplish creating your Victorious Mindset just as I did. And it's important for you to know that you, Reader, "You were created for EXTRAORDINARY." I say that because it's true, there is only one you. Do you know that no one in the world has your exact fingerprint or looks exactly like you. You are unique and created for Extraordinary!

And I have found that the way I got there, and you can too, is through the steps in this book, which are short, simple, and to the point. Each step, as you accomplish it, will move you closer to living the life you've only dreamed of. It's time to start creating some new dreams, or take some of those old ones off the shelf and dust them off.

In this book you will learn how to capture your negative thoughts and replace them with positive thoughts. You will learn how to face your fear and turn it into courage. Remember, thoughts are the beginning of changing your life, and you will need courage to get there.

Each Chapter is a concept that addresses a different area of your life. Each Chapter will be like a 'building block' for the next chapter. I'm a guy who likes things simple, uncomplicated, and easy to understand, so I created *The Victorious Mindset* as a simple step-by-step training system. Your part will be to put in some time and effort to work the steps and be honest with yourself about where you are, and where you want to go.

There are only 2 ways to go through this book, and whichever way you choose, I am right there with you. Just imagine me being right there with you while you read, we are walking this road together my friend. Choose one of the two ways to proceed forward and go for it!

1
Read the book from beginning (Introduction) to the end of the book. Don't make any notes, don't answer any of the questions, don't go watch any of the 'fun' videos I have provided, and believe me, they are fun and funny. When you get to the end of the book, if you found value in what you read, go back to Chapter 2 "Are You Ready?" and do the following:

2
The second way to go through this book is start at the beginning and 'work' through the book, slowly. The Chapters are short to start with, but I want you to consider carefully, what you're reading and how it applies to your life. The answers may not come to you

right away. Some answers may be difficult to think about. Hang in there through those parts, for the purpose is to put them to rest once and for all! Some chapters will take you longer to work through than others. In each chapter I will present to you information, take what applies to you and work with it. Think about how it applies to your life.

VIDEOS: At the end of a chapter you find video hotlinks (not all chapters have them) or URLs, which feature video instructions by me of what you just read. It is not necessary to watch them, but I think they are light, fun, and informative. I want you to enjoy your journey through this book of mine, and I definitely want you to be able to laugh more in life. Laughter is very good!

PERSONAL NOTES SECTION: This is the area you get to write in. This is your workbook so go ahead write in it. Perhaps have a hi-liter handy too, there's some really good stuff in here.

AUTHOR'S CHALLENGE: I, the Author, will present to you, some questions or thoughts to consider and work on. There is no rush. Work on each chapter as long as it takes you to go through it and work it out. Remember, the better the questions you ask yourself, the better the answers you'll come up with.

Chapter 17, "The Daily Power Start and Maintenance System" is something you can either write out long hand or type it up and print it out, to keep with you all the time, seriously. This is the part where you will exercise your mind, a daily routine to keep you on track. This is where your mind will become bigger, better, stronger, and faster as you exercise it daily. I started writing this book in 2009, and as of this writing today five years later, I still use this 'system' daily.

Why? Because this system is still working for me, and my mind is still growing to increasing levels. I have not hit the ceiling and am still reaching for the stars!

Get Physical with Your Mind in Chapter 18 is where you will engage your body right alongside your mind.

Battle Affirmations are in Chapter 19. Affirmations will expand your belief in yourself, your talents, your abilities, your dreams, and your life! Affirmations are best used when said out loud, while you are standing up, and put some effort and passion into it by moving your body – I call them 'power moves'. Whatever you are capable of doing, like: throw your arms out to your sides or up in the air, crouch down bending your knees bouncing up and down a little bit, repeatedly lifting your body up and forward onto the balls of your feet and back down again, lifting your shoulders up-and-down, open and close your hands into fists. Imagine yourself at a sports event and your team just won! Throw your arms up in the air, your excited, celebrate! This is how you will really get your desire going strong, like you want it, you desire it. And if you feel silly doing these power moves, good, laugh at yourself, laughter is good!

Battle Quotes are in Chapter 20. These are like food to your mind. As you read them, say them aloud, repeat them, your mind will remember them and believe them. Your thinking gets stronger and grows, your confidence grows, you will challenge yourself more, and you will start aiming for the stars in the sky. Think about it, if you aim for the stars and miss, you have still reached the sky.

Whatever you do, please don't skip around or skip a whole chapter. Each one is a 'building block' necessary for the next step. Think of it like baking a cake. Can you tell I like sweets? I have put all these ingredients out on the counter for you to make your favorite yummy cake. If you 'skip' any one of the ingredients and don't use it, your cake will not come out to be the best most beautiful yummy cake it could have been. Utilize this book as intended, use its ingredients in order, as requested, have fun with it, enjoy the journey!

DEDICATION

Important People

I dedicate this book to my extraordinary and beautiful wife, Lisa, who takes my breath away. I also dedicate this book to my extraordinary children Brian, Jordan, and Jaydie. They are all amazing miracles in my moments!

FOREWORD

Victorious mindset

Hello, my name is Dr. Phillip R. Aguilar. I have known Richard "Chip" Esajian for over 20 years, not only as a close personal friend but also as a colleague in business, as well as in Ministry work helping people get Set Free! It was my privilege to oversee the marriage of Chip to his beautiful wife, Lisa, and I am truly blessed to call them my friends.

The contents of this book you are about to embark on will revolutionize your whole way of thinking! You will have a new view and a brand new attitude towards each and every day. This book will touch on many topics, one of which is the *choices* that we make, and it will go on to teach you the very importance of understanding the battlefield of the mind. Another is *denial*, which is an obstacle that keeps many people from attaining their goals along with stunting their hope and possibility for a successful future. One of my own personal favorite topics, *acceptance*! This is where you will learn the value of how unique of a person you are, and how amazing it truly is that there is only one YOU! And of course, *forgiveness*, which is a very deep subject nowadays in this world we live in. Until we learn to forgive someone, that person will set-up camp and get free rent in our mind. We need to learn to forgive and live!

The techniques and theories in this book are simplified and explained in such a way that you can easily put them into practice in your own lives immediately; so you don't have to let one more moment go by without having the tools to make your life a transformation as monumental and beautiful as a caterpillar into a butterfly!

Every word of this book will catapult you into the boot camp of life. The bridge we all cross, from immaturity and childhood into adulthood can feel like a 'boot camp' experience. I believe it is discipline, temperance, and a strong mind that helps us persevere through the most difficult and seemingly impossible challenges in this life. This book is far more than information, it is inspiration! You will be inspired to push through your problems and work through otherwise difficult dilemmas with far less confusion and questions, coming out on the other side with many more solutions.

Many books out there have been written targeting self-improvement and self-help issues, but none like this one, it's very different. Richard is real and down-to-earth, with a keep-it-simple approach to teaching us to truly enjoy the journey of life. You will be given affirmations, helping you to create your own 'flavor' that best supports your own personal growth; which will ultimately keep you from settling for less in life. It will also help you from getting dragged into that downward spiral of living we see happening to so many others around us, as well as not allowing yourself to get caught up in the all-consuming neg-ativity that has taken so many of our loved ones down a dark road.

The Victorious Mindset can help you develop a new mindset, acquire new friends, in turn open up a brand new playing field which includes fun, happiness, and a lust for life! In life I have found, we all need coaches to push us toward our goals, friends to support us through the good and bad times, mentors to look up to and get good counsel from, and sponsors to lean on - knowing they have been through similar situations to help guide us in the right direction. By reading this book you will learn what to look for in people, so you can attain all those attributes in your own support crew, to ultimately be the kind of person someone would want on their team!

Since first being introduced to Richard, a young man who was struggling with direction and wanting peace of mind; I have watched him transform into a happy and blessed man. He is making wonderful choices in his life which have brought him all he ever could have dreamed of and then some!

Love, peace and prosperity. Mind, body and soul!

Phillip R. Aguilar,
Dr. of Divinity

ACKNOWLEDGEMENTS

My extremely gifted and caring publisher has let me know how important it is to list the specific names of the people, groups, and organizations that have helped me during the creation of this book. Over the years, I have done my best to let each of these important people know, each and every time we connected with one another, how much I appreciated their contributions. Additionally, I have let them know how much I care about them personally, that I honor who they are, and that I love them. For this section of my book, I have chosen to respect their privacy.

The preparation for this book extends back to my childhood, to all my family, both immediate and extended family members. Throughout my life you've given me so much love, encouragement, support, and respect. I am so grateful that I get to be part of your lives. I honor you for your integrity, character, and loving hearts.

To those who are my friends, who I will call 'family,' and you know who you are; I am grateful, thankful, and appreciative of your kindness, love, counsel, and support (in many ways). I pay honor to all of you who comforted me when I was down, who celebrated with me when I was victorious, and who stood by me in between. I am humbled by the great contributions you've made to my life, and more importantly, in letting me into your lives and calling me 'family.'

There is a select group of generous individuals who personally contributed to this book by assisting me with spelling, sentence construction, and harnessing my thoughts. English may be my first language, but it became obvious to me while writing this book, that I needed help. I thank you for your tactfulness, your patience, and using your valuable personal time to teach me.

Additionally, there are those who read and reread my book drafts through multiple edits and gave me your honest feedback. I thank you for helping me keep the integrity of what I wrote, in the manner and style that I speak, and really being helpful in bringing about a much improved and superb book. I pay respect and honor to you for your contributions. To the dedicated professionals, I thank you for your valuable and significant input, and I am grateful for your expertise.

To all the students who attended my *Victorious Mindset* meetings, seminars, group studies, and various teachings - I thank you for being there, for your whole-hearted contributions, and for participating in letting me be a part of your lives. Each of you is an extraordinary miracle.

There are a group of people I don't know personally, except through 'social media' channels; however, I am appreciative of your efforts to connect with me, in promoting my book and videos, for your honest feedback, and for your continued support. I see more victory for all of us still to come!

I want to honor my truly extraordinary and beautiful wife Lisa. You, I love. I honor all three of my amazing children - Brian, Jordan, and Jaydie. I also honor my dad, mom, and sister, Brandy. One of my greatest inspirations, for the example of a mindset I wanted to have, is my youngest daughter Jaydie who has autism. I see Jaydie as the most pure, happy, loving, innocent soul I have ever experienced on planet earth. She takes my breath away.

During my life before writing this book I was not the type of person who would be considered much of a reader or a writer. Other than the required reading and writing I did in high school, college, and various jobs – the one and only book I ever read consistently, over and over again is the Bible. So when I started writing affirmations and quotes onto index cards, I was surprised at myself. I wondered, "Where did this come from?"

Then I switched to a notebook because there were too many index cards to keep track of. That notebook turned into a typed-up manuscript on my laptop, and miraculously, I had a book. I give the glory and honor to God for putting this book in me, for letting me be the first to read it, and put my name on it. Thank you Jesus!

INTRODUCTION

HOW DID WE GET HERE?

> Create extraordinary happiness from extreme gratefulness, not from financial or circumstantial gain or loss, and build a bridge above anxiety and fear.
>
> Chip Esajian, Motivational Coach

This is a training system for creating a Victorious Mindset and it is possible because of so many people in my life. I'm filled with gratefulness to God, my wife, my children, my family, and friends, who have always believed in me. In addition, I must give thanks and respect to a whole group of people I have not met personally, who have been *great influences[1]* in my life through their books, videos, television programs, and seminars.

I wrote this book to provide others with a simple system comprised of steps to enable a re-programming of their entire belief and thought processes. Going from limited thinking to unlimited thinking, from can't to can, from impossible to possible is what this training system helps others achieve!

I also wrote this book for everyone who desires to step into the command center of their brain where they can take control and create an extraordinary Victorious Mindset!

If you are tired of putting up with yourself. If you are done watching life happen to you. If you are tired of being a victim and if you are tired of being negative, pessimistic, unforgiving, hateful, judgmental, stressed, fearful, anxiety ridden, insecure, etc. – this book is for YOU!

Would you like to be able to create the life you've imagined?

Would you like to create a happiness that gives you chills of excitement anytime you want them?

Would you like to fly higher in life than you ever have?

Would you like to create an extraordinary life that YOU'VE DESIGNED that others will want, rather than a life that keeps sending you spiraling down into "The cave of miseries?"

---

[1] Les Brown, Dale Carnegie, Joel Osteen, Tony Robbins, Jim Rohn, Zig Ziegler.

Are you ready to create a life where all things are possible? To create a life where you float above your circumstances? A life where people are attracted to you and feel elevated in your presence?

Did you say you are **READY**? Oftentimes, you say you're ready, but really are not ready to put in the amount of work, commitment, practice, dedication, and passion it will take to achieve consistent bliss at will.

Are you sure you're ready to free yourself from the *prison* you're living in?

Are you ready to free yourself from the miserable *matrix* mindset you've endured your entire life?

Imagine a life of extraordinary mental freedom, happiness, excitement, forgiveness, gratefulness, thankfulness, victory, and attractiveness. Imagine **YOUR** amazing life where you love who you are. Imagine a life where **YOU** can't wait to give to others, because you are so overflowing with extraordinary happiness and abundance. All **YOU** can think about is who to give to next.

Imagine a life where **YOU** see opportunities and possibilities everywhere you look! Imagine loving who **YOU** are so you can see the *wonderful* in others.

You were created for an extraordinary purpose. There is no one who looks like you! There is no one with the same finger print you have. Your heart is kept beating so you can create a victorious, grateful mindset to move the mountains out of the way of your dreams!

All the quotes and affirmations you will read in this workbook were inspired and written as I created my Victorious Mindset.

Buckle your seat belt and enjoy the ride, as I share my Victorious Mindset system with you, my extraordinary friend!

AUTHOR'S CHALLENGE

Read and consider the question listed below and fill in your answers. This helps provide a working tool and resource for your continued growth toward YOUR Victorious Mindset!

1. List here why you are ready and willing to change your thought life so you can live a more victorious life:

_____

_____

_____

_____

_____

_____

_____

CHAPTER ONE

MY JOURNEY

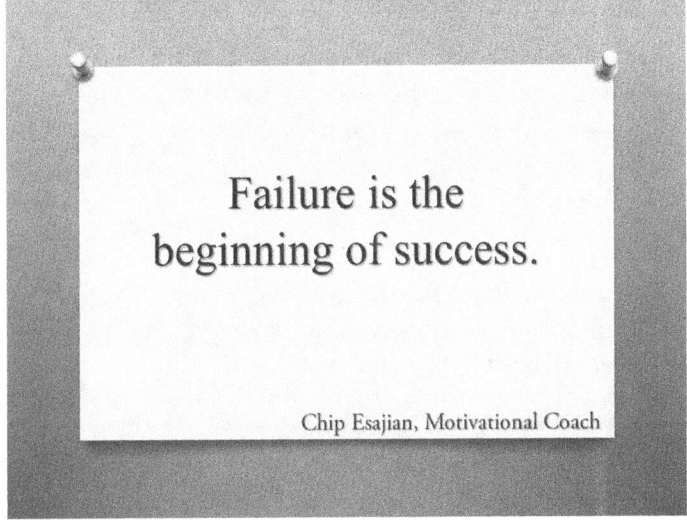

Failure is the
beginning of success.

Chip Esajian, Motivational Coach

Before I share more about *The Victorious Mindset* power system, it is important for you to know about me and my past. In this way, you'll understand I am an ordinary person. I created my Victorious Mindset while living with my wife in my mother-in-law's mobile home. I'm not a doctor, psychologist, therapist, or pastor. I did not graduate from an institution of higher-learning with a Bachelor or Master degree, but "The Victorious Mindset Training System" is endorsed by many professionals who have.

As a matter of fact, I only completed six months of college, which was enough torture for me. I was a whiner. I complained. I was ungrateful, negative, selfish, jealous, and covetous. And, I was also an egotistical and angry person on the inside, but I faked it on the outside for such a long time, setting myself up for many failures. I can't begin to tell you how much crap I fed myself daily while remaining in denial concerning the truth about my life.

I knew I really didn't have much to offer anyone, but the funny part was, I chose to believe my own lies: . . . *I'm a great guy and people should like me; if they don't, something is wrong with them . . . it certainly isn't me.* In my mind, I'd even say, *How can this person not like me?*

Today, I'm thankful to have the ability to share real feelings; there is a freedom in sharing real thoughts with readers like YOU!

An important aspect of "The Victorious Mindset Training System" is just this, to free your own mind as I have done. It works! Give it a shot.

Growing up in Fresno, California, I was raised in a normal (dysfunctional) family filled with insecurities, worries, anxieties, and fears. Due to this fact, I developed much insecurity in my thought life at a very young age. Of course, I attended school like everyone else; however, I was held back in 1st grade because I couldn't sit still, which threw the initial weight on my internal thought[ii] insecurity blanket. We attended church on Sunday, but it really bored me. At age nine, I

[ii]   For this title, think of the internal thought self as the subconscious self or self-image.

began to play the trumpet and also started playing tennis.

As a young man, I also wanted to play football, but my mother said, "No." With football being such a pivotal sport for a guy – it seemed important to me to team up; so, what can I say? Thanks to my mom, I still have a good back and knees!

An incident from growing up, which sticks out in my mind took place when I was nine. I had developed a crush on a cute girl in the 6th grade. I liked her so much I wrote her a love note and gave it to her with a little plastic ring I got out of a gum ball machine. When she opened the note and read it, she threw the plastic ring on the ground and ran off laughing. She turned me down. I didn't think it was funny and from that day forward I allowed such experiences to add to my insecurities and build internal thought self-doubt.

High school was where my pride, ego, insecurities, and emotions really began expressing themselves. While I felt I was pretty normal, I maintained a constant need to compare myself to others. At the time, I wore thick rimmed glasses and had a big nose.

In high school, I began to really take notice of the physical differences between myself and other students at my school. I imagine you may do this too. I had no clue what being content and at peace meant. It is sad and peculiar how in high school, we think we are the only one experiencing insecurities and inner turmoil.

Well, I made it through high school. And, I was actually able to travel the world with our school jazz band. We marched in the *Ronald Regan Inaugural* parade. I also managed to play varsity tennis and graduated with average grades. After graduation, I didn't know what I wanted to do with my life. After only six months of study, I dropped out of college – it just wasn't for me, which isn't to suggest it is not for you. I believe college is for some, but not everyone.

This left me with no clue what I was going to do with my life. I wasn't happy working routine normal jobs, but what recent graduate is? My worry was, I felt out of place and that was scary and this also added to my insecurities, doubts, and fears with only 19 years of life on planet earth at the time. Perhaps you are experiencing the same challenges?

It was at this time, the most amazing thing happened in my life. While at the gym with a friend, I was introduced to the head dancer and owner of a male exotic dance group! I'd heard about the dance group previous to meeting the owner, as the only exotic male dance group in our city – everyone knew about them. After sharing some conversation with him, I was asked to audition. The very next day I did and suddenly, I was a male exotic dancer.

For nearly a year I danced with the group. During this year my confidence (ego) really grew (blew up)! Virtually overnight, I went from dud to stud, both in my head and in real life. Girls were all around me and it was an extremely intense ego boost! Then my dream came to me! I'll move to Hollywood, get a job at Chippendales, and become a movie star! Today it sounds funny just saying it.

And, I did just that. I went to Hollywood, made connections, and landed a gig with Chippendales. Then, I began taking acting lessons! All of a sudden within one year's time, I completely changed my life from drab to fab. It was an impossible fantasy come true and it was gaining momentum!

Working my way up the ladder at Chippendales, I became one of the MC's (master of ceremonies) and a top professional dancer. At the same time, I cured some of my self-doubt by getting a nose job! YES! I FINALLY DID IT! I got rid of my honker and my ego continued to grow.

Afterward, a former child star actress came into my life and she said she saw something in me. This was great to hear after many years of self-doubt and internal disbelief. She became my acting manager.

Everything was right where I wanted it to be. Life was perfect. At least, it was in my mind. I knew I was on my way! During the day, I practiced acting and went to auditions. At night, I worked at Chippendales to pay my way!

Being a male dancer, envisioning my Block Buster movies, was a fantasy way beyond what I'd ever imagined. I was too cool for school.

To make a long story short: after five years of pushing my dreams forward, I was in an acting showcase, which my manager organized and produced. She invited many Hollywood connections including a key stakeholder from a major studio to view my acting debut.

It was my big break! I was fired up! I was totally confident this was it; everything I'd ever fathomed to dream of was in my grasp. After the showcase my manager told me her producer friend loved my performance! How great is that! And, I was up for a part in a big feature film, the catch was the studios wanted me to quit working at Chippendales and I didn't appreciate the request.

This is where my story turns yet again, and the rug was pulled out from under me; I love it when that happens.

So, I quit working with Chippendales. This was like going cold turkey from the most addictive drug imaginable and I went through heavy withdrawals. I went from living in fantasyland, with a dream job, with gorgeous women all around me; to the cold reality of working a real job. The women were gone. My confidence was gone and I lost my edge.

My foundation was built on this huge and false fantasy platform, but I didn't realize there was a trap door below me! When the attention subsided, the trap door opened and I fell through it. My confidence: GONE. Lost mentally; I couldn't act anymore. I no longer knew who I was! The helium ego balloon I'd been sporting around . . . burst! This left me confused and shocked and I left town without telling anyone where I was headed.

I moved to Orange County California from Hollywood and stayed in a friend's warehouse. Then, I slept in a tent inside the warehouse for an entire year.

It was a humbling experience. I felt destroyed, lost, and distraught beyond anything ever experienced in my life previous to that point in time! It was a nightmare I wanted to wake up from. My brain was mush and I was a train wreck.

To make ends meet, I began selling casters and wheels and welding shopping carts in my friend's warehouse where I lived. Yes, I slept in a tent on the roof of an office just below the ceiling of the warehouse. Each night, I climbed up the fork lift to get into my tent. Emotionally, it was as if I was out at sea trying to remain afloat and I was running out of strength.

Here is where my story takes an unexpected turn. After about a year of warehouse living, at the lowest point in my entire life, smelling dust with every breath I was 26 years old and ready to give up. I'll never forget the day I was so miserable and hollowed out inside, that I fell to my knees. I broke down and cried and uttered this prayer:

"God if you are listening. If you love me and really have a purpose for my life, I'll try you. I've tried everything else and I don't have any more quarters left to put in the machine. But you've got to show me somehow that you've heard my prayer today; something has to happen! You've got to get me somewhere that will show me how real you are. You have to do a miracle in my life. But I'm not wearing a suit, going to a boring church, or cutting my hair (Yes, I had long hair at that time.).

Show me that you've heard my prayer!"

Now, I didn't see stars . . . the room didn't light up, but something was different. Two weeks later, while at a gym I frequented, a man came in the gym I had never seen before. He walked over to me and started talking about God. He told me about a place where I could find out more about God if it was my desire. I looked up at this strange, but happy guy. At that moment, I had a feeling my prayer had been heard and I was filled with hope once again.

A week later, my new found friend took me to this warehouse, which was packed with people. It was a church. When I walked through the doors, a rush came over me and a peace I had never felt before seized the moment! It was simply amazing. I knew, right then I was at home. This opened up an entire new journey in life. I had new hope and excitement. It was then; I knew our creator had a purpose for me and my life.

A month later, I asked my new found friend if he had ever been back to the gym. He told me "NO." He stated, "That day was the first and only time I'd ever been to the gym." I know it sounds hokey, but it is true; it was a modern day miracle for me. We each have our own journey and beliefs, but this is me sharing my story, you may have a different story filled with unique miracles of your own!

Soon after, while still living and working in the warehouse, I met a young lady while at lunch with a friend. She liked "me", despite the fact I lived in a warehouse and I was amazed. A few months later, I married her and we raised three wonderful children.

During this time, we used the house we lived in to help the warehouse church ministry I'd found. We took in the homeless and aided those just out of prison. We assisted individuals who wanted to be set free from drugs. Basically, we helped others gain new beginnings in their lives.

For a couple of years I provided ministerial assistance, and then transitioned to living just with my family. At this time, I became a car detailer. And, after a couple more years, got into the mortgage business as a loan officer; at eight years of marriage, my wife and I went through a divorce and again, I was caught completely off guard. With no idea my wife was unhappy; I realized I'd been living in denial believing everything was great. I thought I was a good dad and husband. Reality set in and my life returned to the living nightmare. To move away from my wife and children was now, by far, the most difficult thing I had ever experienced in life. If there was hell on earth, I believed I was in it. Being hurt, broken, angry, jealous, miserable, and empty among many other emotions at the time, I faced coming out of denial and began to SEE who I was. I didn't like what I saw.

Reality slapped me in the face and I knew there was no one to blame but myself. The responsibility was mine and I needed to find a way through the darkness I'd created. When I faced my mistakes honestly, I realized I wasn't a great husband or father. And this realization rocked me to the core. For a lengthy amount of time, I cried every day. I sobbed until my insides were hollowed out and it was a pain of self-realization I wouldn't wish on anyone.

Healing took years and during those years, I was wise enough to avoid dating. I determined to stay away from women. In my mind, I had nothing of value to offer them except more misery. I was not about to rebound into another relationship so I could put all my garbage in someone else's yard.

So, I decided to move in with friends from the warehouse church ministry I had found years earlier. I was broken and they embraced me and nursed me back to life. In the first year post-divorce, my children moved to another state with their mother and that was very difficult to endure. I learned to be grateful in just being able to talk to my children on the telephone and to have the opportunity to visit them every few months. Gratefulness, humility, and patience became my goal. Daily I worked on being grateful so I wouldn't complain about things I couldn't change.

Between staying away from getting in any new relationships and going through a healing process, I began to learn who Chip Esajian really is. I wanted happiness. So, I began to work on forgiveness and letting go of a past I could not change. A light at the end of the tunnel emerged even though I didn't see one. Month-by-month my pain subsided. Once again, self-confidence arose. Emotional pain from the past had caused me to learn from my mistakes and failures. I faced them. I embraced them.

It was approximately two-and-a-half years post-divorcement, when I was ready to be single forever that my current, beautiful and extraordinary wife walked into my life. And, I wasn't looking for a relationship, but our friends set us up; so, I asked her out. We went on one date and we were married three weeks later. Today, we continue to have one of the greatest marriages on planet earth. My Lisa is the *wind beneath my wings* that God gave me. Being married to Lisa, makes me want to be a better man. As a step-mom, she loves my children as her own and they love her.

Interestingly enough, we get along very well with my ex-wife who is a great mother to the wonderful children we share.

Still, finances remained very tight for me; there were months where we were behind a month or two. I worried a lot. It was very troubling not to have enough money, because my happiness remained attached to financial and circumstantial gain or loss at the time.

Four years into our wonderful marriage, I took another major stand in my life journey. In our garage one evening, I looked at my wife and said, "Honey, I am sick and tired, of being sick and tired of having my brain run my life and not being able to do anything about it except whine about it. Here I am, never having gone a day without food in my life, and yet I still worry about finances, have unforgiveness and bitterness toward others. I worry about my mistakes from the past and have anxieties about the future, which has my present paralyzed."

This is where I decided to put my foot down. I was done putting up with myself and my stinking thinking! I wanted happiness! I didn't want to worry about anything regardless of circumstances. I knew I had been given a brain to think with. It wasn't until that very moment where I made the choice to give myself a serious check-up from the neck up that I understood the extraordinary victorious mindset. It was then, "The Victorious Mindset Training System" gave birth. All things were possible and I knew I could create a life where regardless of external circumstances; I could be living in a kingdom of extraordinary wonderful in my mind!

I set out to learn how to get control of my thoughts and with complete and full determination I strove to learn how to live a more victorious, exciting, and purposeful life comprised of personal choice and individual design each and every day regardless of circumstances!

And so my victorious journey started! I began developing the steps included in this training guide. I powered up my mind to live the life I imagined. I'm an easy-going kind of guy and I like things simple. So I developed a system, which worked by simple practice. The system I created, "The Victorious Mindset Training System," is what I used to develop a grateful, thankful, abundant, exciting, victorious, happy, and fulfilling life.

Life for me today is extraordinary. Life is powerful. I make the choice to not allow *can't* in my Victorious Mindset arsenal.

Creating a Victorious Mindset allows me to enjoy my thought life in a new exciting way. I have created more value in others' lives by creating more value in mine!

The world has opened up to me and I'm courageously engaging every bit of it!

I'm living the extraordinary life I've imagined, and I'm so excited to share it with YOU!

AUTHOR'S CHALLENGE

Read and consider the question listed below and fill in your answers. This helps provide a working tool and resource for your continued growth toward YOUR Victorious Mindset!

1. When looking over your own journey up to this point, do you see parts of your life that could have been extremely different if you would have had a more Victorious Mindset of gratitude? Note some of them here:

_____

_____

_____

_____

"To have all you want, you must first see all you have, then you'll realize you have more than most."

Chip Esajian, Motivational Coach

CHAPTER TWO

ARE YOU READY?

Are you sure you are ready to live the life you've imagined?

Dance with your

FEAR

until it turns into courage.

Chip Esajian, Motivational Coach

Are you sure you are sick and tired, of being sick and tired of your run amuck mind led by its emotions?

Are you tired of having the movie screen in your mind running nonstop with all your fears, worries, insecurities, bitterness, anger, jealousy, anxiety, depression, sadness, unforgiveness, and etc.?

Have you finally said, "Enough is enough?"

If your answer is "YES" then you have made the wisest and most important *choice* of your life.

What could be MORE IMPORTANT in life than creating extraordinary value in you, to give to others? NOTHING!

It's amazing there are no classes in school for what you're about to learn. There is a specific order to the steps to maximize your results. If you follow the order of steps in this book you can achieve your goals in a much shorter time period, than if you skip steps.

Ok, now that you have committed to living the life you've only imagined, there are a few rules!

AUTHOR'S CHALLENGE

Read and consider the questions listed below and fill in your answers. This helps provide a working tool and resource for your continued growth toward YOUR Victorious Mindset!

1. Why am I ready for a more victorious life?

   _____

   _____

   _____

2. Why am I committed to doing the work needed to create my Victorious Mindset?

   _____

   _____

   _____

3. I believe greater things are in store for me, such as:

   _____

   _____

   _____

CHAPTER THREE

RULES

BE VICTORIOUS!

Chip Esajian, Motivational Coach

RULE NUMBER ONE

Read this book all the way through as many times as you like, but only work on one step at a time in the order the steps are written.

You must surrender, believe, take action, and achieve each step before trying to jump ahead. Going from Step 1 to Step 10 without working on the other steps will become frustrating. Every step in the training system builds on the former step and is very important to the complete process! You must learn how to fly a plane before you can pilot one!

RULE NUMBER TWO

For the best results, you must commit to working "The Victorious Mindset Training System" 24/7. This is not a book you read once, and then you're changed!

"Amazing victories, require you to welcome Amazing battles courageously."

Chip Esajian, Motivational Coach

Treat this book as if it's part of your body and person. Where you go, it goes! Take this matter very seriously. I do, and so should you. **THIS IS A VITAL PART OF THE PROCESS**! Take this book wherever you go!

RULE NUMBER THREE

You are now on a journey of choice and change. For some of you, certain steps will be easier than others.

The steps require practice. As you practice changing your beliefs about what is possible for your life, you begin to change. The quicker you embrace change in your life, the sooner you experience positive results.

RULE NUMBER FOUR

Have fun on this journey! You will go through all kinds of emotions as you move closer to taking back control of the command center of your mind! Focus on having fun on this journey of victory.

RULE NUMBER FIVE

There are two choices in life regarding self-discovery and a Victorious Mindset:

1. Living a life of scarcity
2. Living a life of extraordinary abundance

First, you must blow up all the bridges which lead to giving up!

There is **NO QUITING!** There is **NO GIVING UP!** Seriously, is there anything else in your life as important as building true happiness? It takes just as much energy and work to be miserable as it takes to create a Victorious Mindset. Even if you already feel "victorious" using the techniques in this training system, they will still strengthen and add to your current self-awareness.

Many people are going through life with blinders on. And, many don't even realize this. Up to this point in your life, you 'may' have practiced becoming the person you are today with or without blinders. Seeing victory as your destination and accepting nothing less – is what you deserve!

Read this affirmation out loud with consistent, excited passion and desire!

"Today, I choose to create a powerful mindset of grateful, thankful, forgiving, loving, appreciative, exciting, wonderful, inspiring, victorious thoughts, because I will accept nothing short of an amazing, victorious, abundant life."

RULE NUMBER SIX

"Can't" is no longer in your vocabulary. You must remove it.

You are now the "can man" or the "can woman." Whether you believe you can or can't do something, you are correct! You can do anything you **SET YOUR MIND** to!

You will go from limited to unlimited beliefs as you clear the road to an extraordinary life that is awaiting you to join it! What you believe is possible, you will be able to achieve.

RULE NUMBER SEVEN

You need to write down your goals and a plan of action of how you're going to get to each goal along your journey! This book will assist you in creating the mindset you will need to courageously go after your goals.

You need to set time frames for your Victorious Mindset accomplishments, so you can see your progress! **First**, you must know where you're starting your journey from. You **MUST** be honest with yourself, evaluate where you are at in your current mindset.

Second, you need to know where you're going. You need to know your destination. **Third**, you need to write down a plan on how you will get there. When you run MapQuest you have to know the start point and the destination, before the map is laid out for you – the same here.

You need to set short range goals at daily, weekly, monthly, 3 month, 6 month, and 1 year intervals, etc.

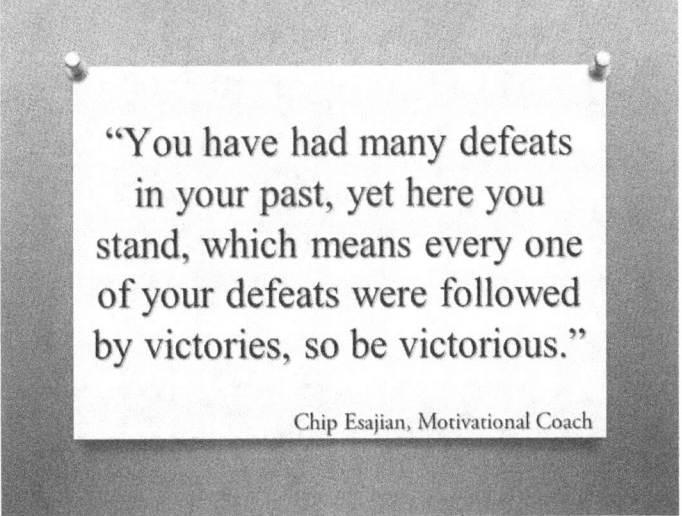

"You have had many defeats in your past, yet here you stand, which means every one of your defeats were followed by victories, so be victorious."

Chip Esajian, Motivational Coach

Write goals you intend to see happen in your life in 3 to 5 years; these are long range goals.

It is important to count "**WINS**" instead of "**LOSSES**" along your journey in life. Focus on **WINS** in everything you do. Counting wins rather than losses, becomes easier once your starting point and destination are written down and ingrained in your training system practices.

Set a goal for yourself for when you would like to have all the steps initially achieved by. Set goals that push you and command your attention!

RULE NUMBER EIGHT

You must **TAKE ACTION**! Thinking about something without applying action does nothing. Choose to become a person who **TAKES ACTION** immediately!

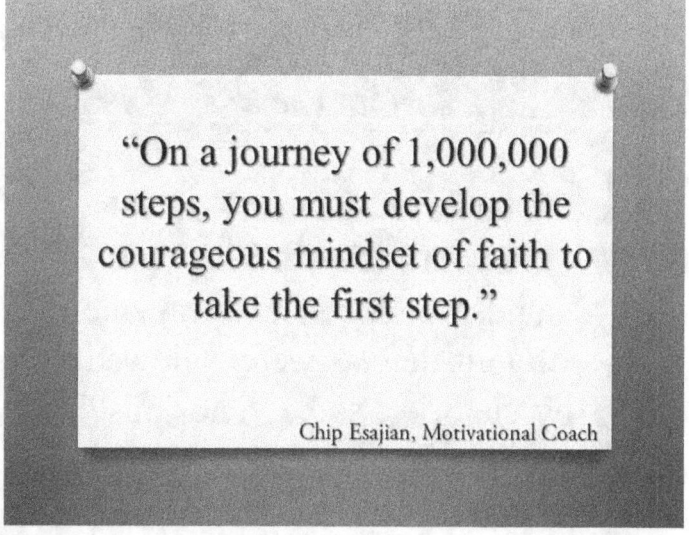

> "On a journey of 1,000,000 steps, you must develop the courageous mindset of faith to take the first step."
>
> Chip Esajian, Motivational Coach

ACTION is replacing procrastination in your life! When you started reading this book – you took ACTION! From this point forward, focus on taking ACTION instead of thinking about it.

RULE NUMBER NINE

The Victorious Mindset is about tapping into the parts of your mind you haven't exercised on a regular basis, if at all. It's not about changing outside circumstances! It's about changing the perception and view you hold for yourself, and the rest of the world. You are learning to create happiness from internal gratefulness and not from financial and monetary gain. A person who bases happiness on financial and monetary gain or loss lives in a constant state of anxiety and fear of loss, because these are not qualities, they are circumstances.

The Victorious Mindset is about creating a mindset, which allows you to tread above circumstance. As you create a victorious and abundant mindset, you begin to shed the need for greed. You won't focus on what you don't have, losing what you do have, or having more than you currently have.

Instead, victorious abundance no one can take from you will be created in your heart, mind, and being. This is more fulfilling than being handed a million dollars!

CHAPTER THREE VIDEO[3]

The link provided below, will bring you to a video visual summary of what you just read. It is a fun and quick demonstration, by me personally, to be used as a working tool and resource for your continued growth toward YOUR Victorious Mindset!

http://youtu.be/pmxmPOZYCQg

---

[3]   "The author could have these videos remastered, but wanted to remain true to the realism of this initial training system and therefore, included videos as is. Some have slippage, but are still understandable. In the future, a remastered version will be available for purchase."

CHAPTER THREE
PERSONAL NOTES SECTION FOR THE
"RULES"

AUTHOR'S CHALLENGE

Read and consider the question listed below and fill in your answers. This helps provide a working tool and resource for your continued growth toward YOUR Victorious Mindset!

1. Will I commit to implementing these rules into my own journey of creating a more victorious me?

    YES or **NO** (circle one)

    If "No" what's holding you back from committing?

    _____

    _____

    _____

    _____

    _____

    _____

    _____

    _____

    _____

    _____

    _____

    _____

CHAPTER FOUR

THE greatest moment in YOUR Life

> Start looking at life with unlimited beliefs by believing all things are possible!
>
> Chip Esajian, Motivational Coach

Now it's time to find your destination! You will need to revisit your past to remember the most incredible, happy, exciting, moment of your life. This is to give you an idea of the direction you're headed.

WHAT WAS THE MOST INCREDIBLE

MOMENT OF YOUR LIFE?

Do you remember a time in your life when you were incredibly excited? A time when you were full of unbelievable joy and peace beyond all understanding? A time where you had chills of incredible happiness, which lifted you off the ground and held you in a place of complete abundance? You didn't see it coming. You didn't know how you got there. You didn't know how long it would last, but you knew it was too good too last! Then it was gone.

How would you like to create abundance anytime you want? With "The Victorious Mindset Training System," you will! If you have desire and passion to live your imagined life, using this simple and complete system, you will be enabled to create, maintain, and continue to build an amazing life filled with extraordinary abundance!

Recreate through the goal of "incredible excitement" I mentioned earlier in this chapter, as your destination to give you the fuel to create the mindset to take the first step on your journey of many!

CHAPTER FOUR
PERSONAL NOTES SECTION FOR "THE GREATEST MOMENT IN YOUR LIFE"

AUTHOR'S CHALLENGE

Your turn to write it out, in detail, the story about what is was for you or how you would want it to be, of...

1. Your **GREATEST MOMENT**:

_____

_____

_____

_____

_____

_____

_____

_____

_____

_____

_____

_____

_____

_____

CHAPTER FIVE

Let's Dance With 'Fear' For A Moment!

Fear: A distressing emotion aroused by impending danger, evil, pain, etc., whether the threat is real or imagined; concern or anxiety.

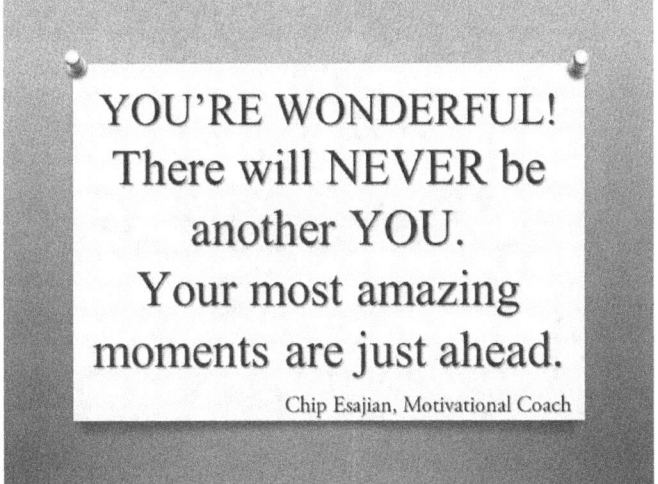

YOU'RE WONDERFUL!
There will NEVER be
another YOU.
Your most amazing
moments are just ahead.

Chip Esajian, Motivational Coach

Have you ever asked yourself, 'What is fear?' Fear is false evidence appearing real. Fear is something that has been instilled in us since we can remember! Fear is nothing more than a combination of worry, anxiety, doubt, confusion, insecurity, and many other intertwined mixed feelings, that occur when we are faced with something we're not ready for, or don't want to face!

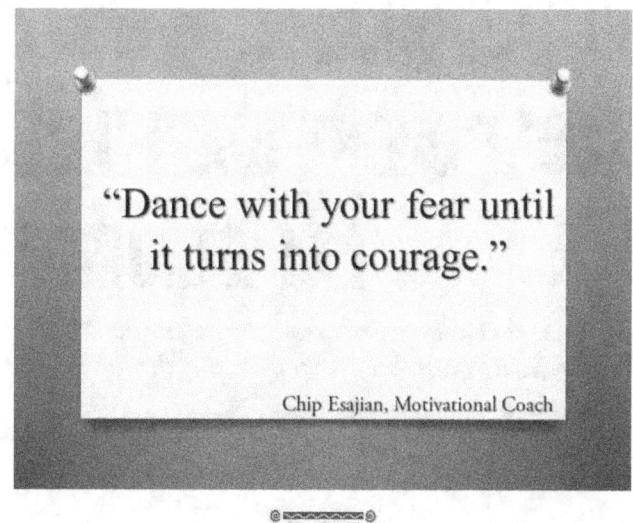

"Dance with your fear until it turns into courage."

Chip Esajian, Motivational Coach

"What you focus on expands, and that, you become."

Chip Esajian, Motivational Coach

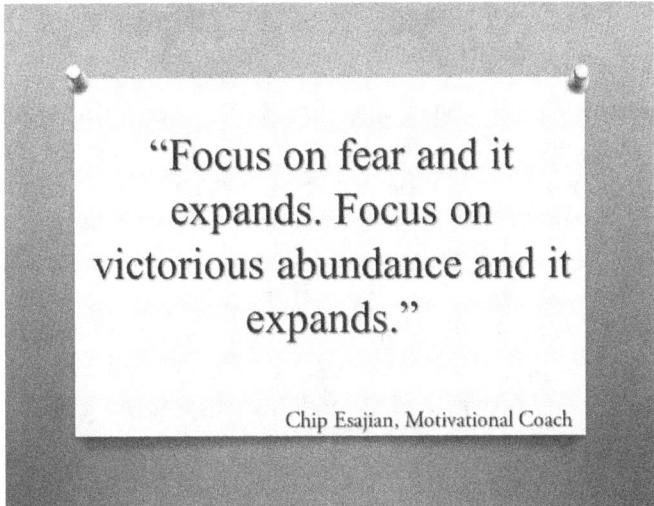

"Focus on fear and it expands. Focus on victorious abundance and it expands."

Chip Esajian, Motivational Coach

"Fear is false evidence appearing real, so engage your mind and blow through your fears with courage."

Chip Esajian, Motivational Coach

Are you ready for the **TRUTH**? Fear is nothing more than an emotion of an illusionary thought you created! Yes, you create fear. Why? Because your mind cannot handle the situations you are going through at the time you are fearful.

From a very young age, you have been programmed with certain fears from all the people's lives you have been a part of. Whether they were real or imagined fears, a lot of them have stayed with you all these years. Those types of fears turned an ant into a giant monster. That fear has kept you from living courageously, because of the possibility of failure. Fear can keep you from stepping out of the boat of life, to walk on waters of the unknown, which leads to extraordinary success, happiness, and abundance.

Fear paralyzes the human mind, and keeps you in a defensive state. You get fearful when finances are threatened. Fear is the backbone supporting disbelief, anxiety, anger, jealousy, and other insecurities you have built into your belief system. Fear causes belief limitations. This system gives you the necessary tools to unlock the doors in your mind to build incredible courageous unlimited beliefs.

The reason I separate fear from the other steps is because fear is the main emotion paralyzing you from accomplishing anything! You're either practicing scarcity or victorious abundance in your life. There is no middle ground. For example, have you ever tried to stand right in the middle of a teeter totter and try to balance it to stay even? It's not possible. One side will always be higher than the other. Where you focus your weight is the side you will move towards. You are either focusing and practicing scarcity or victorious abundance in your life.

Consider you have practiced being fearful of venturing into the unknown for fear of failure. In this state of mind, you are always losing ground and slipping further into mental paralysis. My friend, it's time to get control of your mind and face your fears courageously until they dissolve and disappear before your eyes! Dance with your fear until it turns to courage! Push through your fears! On the other side, amazing victory awaits you.

Face your fears and analyze them. When you look closely, you will see your fear for what it is, an illusion that is not real that you have created. Face your fears and they will dissolve. Fear cannot stand up to close scrutiny! Fear is nothing more than a thought you have assigned an emotion, which keeps you from living the life you've imagined. Boldly turn off the auto-pilot in your mind, and get control so you can fly where you've only imaged you could be.

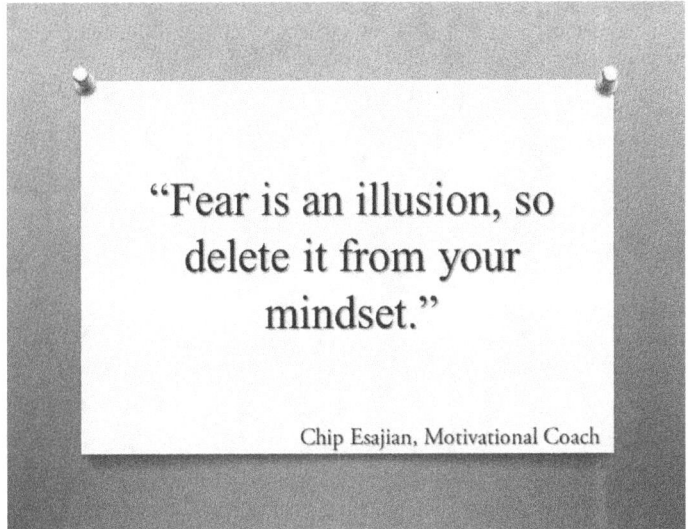

"Fear is an illusion, so delete it from your mindset."

Chip Esajian, Motivational Coach

LIFE WILL NEVER BE THE SAME!

And, fear will fall to the wayside!

Your ultimate destination is living the **EXTRAORD-INARY** abundant, victorious life in your mind that you've only imagined. It will far surpass anything you've ever done. It is the most important journey you will ever take. It will open up a whole new life you never knew was possible or reachable.

People spend their whole lives focusing and working on things in their life that don't even come a close second to working on their minds, towards building a victorious abundant mindset that can elevate their lives to new amazing heights at lightning speed. **THE MOST IMPORTANT THING IN YOUR LIFE YOU SHOULD BE FOCUSSING ON IS BUILDING AN ABUNDANT VICTORIOUS MINDSET!** Why would you settle for anything less than a happy life? Especially when it is no harder than the life you've been practicing.

ARE YOU READY TO SEE A WHOLE NEW WORLD?

"When you change
who you are, doors of
opportunities appear
that you never knew existed."

Chip Esajian, Motivational Coach

CHapter Five videos[4]

The links provided below, will bring you to a video visual summary of what you just read. It is a fun and quick demonstration, by me personally, to be used as a working tool and resource for your continued growth toward YOUR Victorious Mindset!

Fear, Part 1:
http://youtu.be/tf-pwHn7JTo

Fear, Part 2:
http://youtu.be/LsX2E8O1sXA

---

[4] "The author could have these videos remastered, but wanted to remain true to the realism of this initial training system and therefore, included videos as is. Some have slippage, but are still understandable. In the future, a remastered version will be available for purchase."

CHAPTER FIVE PERSONAL NOTES "LET'S DANCE WITH FEAR FOR A MOMENT"

_____

_____

_____

_____

_____

_____

_____

_____

_____

_____

_____

_____

_____

_____

_____

_____

_____

_____

_____

_____

_____

_____

_____

AUTHOR'S CHALLENGE

Read and consider the question listed below and fill in your answers. This helps provide a working tool and resource for your continued growth toward YOUR Victorious Mindset!

1. What fears do I need to dance with until they turn into courage?

_____

_____

_____

_____

_____

_____

_____

_____

_____

_____

_____

_____

CHAPTER SIX

CHOICE

Choice: An act or instance of choosing; the right, power or opportunity to choose.

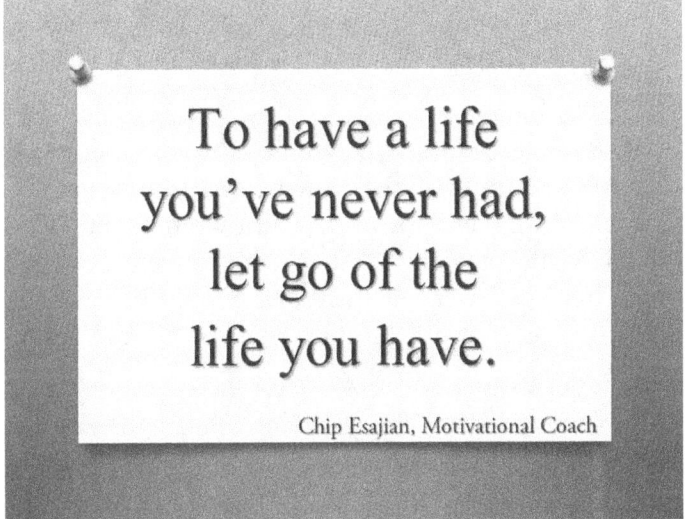

To have a life
you've never had,
let go of the
life you have.

Chip Esajian, Motivational Coach

STEP NUMBER ONE

Y ou have decided enough is enough. You are now making the 'choice' that you're done putting up with yourself.

Did you know the average person makes well over 1,000 choices every day? Some choices you make are bigger than others. All of these choices affect your life, and have molded you into the person you are today. Your choices have become habitual.

Small choices affect you in certain ways, and bigger choices affect you in other ways. For example, you can turn the rudder of a large ship, just a small degree and completely change the destination of a 1,000 mile journey. A person with a limited belief mindset is going to end up in a completely different place than a person with an unlimited belief mindset. Their choices are completely different. Your thoughts have the power to send you spiraling down into the depths of scarcity or to send you soaring up into the unlimited heights of abundance.

All the choices you make come from the thought life you've chosen to allow, which come from your belief system. You have practiced your own thought life and you have become good at it. When you were a child you may have experienced situations in your life that were out of your control. But now that you are old enough, you can make your own choices.

The first step is making a choice to change. You have made the choice you want a different life. You desire a life you've only imagined. Today, you are ready to create a life where you can turn on the power of energy, happiness, excitement, and extraordinary abundance!

A life that holds the amazing purpose you were created for. By your choice today, you are giving yourself the opportunity for an amazing, breathtaking tomorrow.

Read this affirmation out loud with consistent, excited passion and desire!

"Right now, I choose to engage my mind, capture and replace my thoughts and open the door for miracles,

*through belief and faith, with consistent practice of my
new wonderful mindset."*

CHaPTer six viDeos⁵

The links provided below, will bring you to a video
visual summary of what you just read. It is a fun and
quick demonstration, by me personally, to be used as a
working tool and resource for your continued growth
toward YOUR Victorious Mindset!

Choice, Part 1:
http://youtu.be/XYQHlT46XgU

Choice, Part 2:
http://youtu.be/ge_5Fd9opQQ

---

5 " The author could have these videos remastered, but wanted to remain true to the
realism of this initial training system and therefore, included videos as is. Some have
slippage, but are still understandable. In the future, a remastered version will be
available for purchase."

CHAPTER SIX PERSONAL NOTES FOR "CHOICE"

_____

_____

_____

_____

_____

_____

_____

_____

_____

_____

_____

_____

_____

_____

_____

_____

_____

AUTHOR'S CHALLENGE

Read and consider the questions listed below and fill in your answers. This helps provide a working tool and resource for your continued growth toward YOUR Victorious Mindset!

1. Do I choose to make the choice to change my thought life?
   YES or **NO** (circle one)

   If "No" what's holding you back from committing?

   _____

   _____

   _____

   _____

   _____

   _____

2. What are some of the benefits of changing my thought life?

   _____

   _____

   _____

   _____

   _____

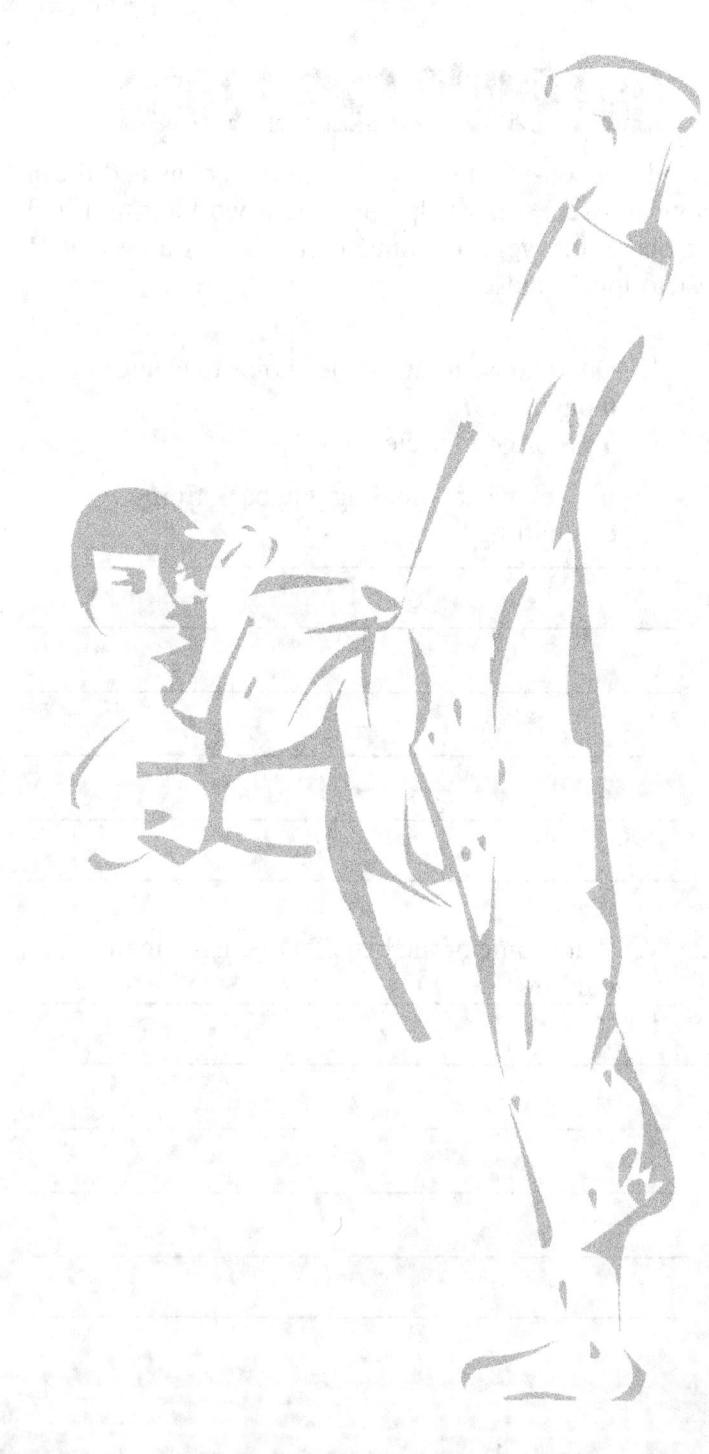

CHAPTER SEVEN

DENIAL

Denial: Refusal to recognize or acknowledge psychology. An unconscious defense mechanism used to reduce anxiety by denying thoughts, feelings, or facts that are consciously intolerable.

> You're one thought away from a wonderful day.
>
> ~
>
> Change your thoughts and you'll change your day!
>
> Chip Esajian, Motivational Coach

STEP NUMBER TWO

You have chosen to get out of 'denial'. Here is an example of being in denial: "It's my families' fault I'm the way I am." You now have to acknowledge you are responsible for the choices you've made. No one else is to blame for where you are in your life right now! Keep in mind:

There are things that were dictated to you at a young age that weren't in your control, such as 'You will never amount to anything,' 'You're fat,' 'You're ugly,' 'You're stupid,' etc. These comments created a false image you patterned life after. You may have been physically harmed at a young age, which was out of your control. But now you are old enough to bring these heavy internal conflicts to the surface and let them go once and for all. Your past is only alive in your mind. This training system teaches you how to let go of a painful past, which no longer exists except in your memory!

Here is the reality . . . you have stuffed so much garbage into the "painful past closet" of your mind; you have chosen to forget most of it. The reality is you're not only in the back of the "painful past closet." You are pinned to the back wall of the closet by all of your past negative thoughts, unforgiveness, and bitterness which you have stored up over time.

This is why you are haunted with painful memories, which pop out at you every so often and run across the movie screen of your mind. All of these negative thoughts and situations you have stuffed are holding you back from realizing your extraordinary purpose that you were created for.

It's time to get out of the closet. Now, how do you do it?

Do you blame others for the situations you have gotten yourself into? Or, should I ask you if you are even aware of the fact you blame others for where you are in life today? Have you been in denial you have a free will choice over every decision you make? It doesn't matter if someone else advised you or not about the choice you should have made. You still had the final say-so to make that choice.

The real question is, do you blame anyone for anything which has happened in your past? If you trusted someone, and they burnt you, did you wrong, disrespected you, cheated on you, cheated you, lied to you, offended you, and etc. ultimately it was still your choice to put trust in them in the first place.

If you blame someone you worked with, your boss, a boyfriend, girlfriend, husband, wife, friend or family member for something bad happening in your life, you're never going to move forward one inch.

It is time to **TAKE RESPONSIBILTY** for every decision in your life, which has led you to this point! You are now old enough and have the free will to make your own choices.

NO BUT'S about it!

Remember you're going for extraordinary abundance in your life.

If you want total freedom from your mental bondage, you have to go back in your past and honestly think about every situation you don't think was your fault. And, because of your passion to free your mind, you must (play by play) walk through your actions of each situation from your past. Even if you went through the most extreme of situations that weren't your fault, you can now choose to let go of a past that no longer exists.

This step will take some work, so get to it, and be very honest with yourself about the entire part you played in each relationship that you have bitterness and unforgiveness in.

If you're feeling pain while you're going through this step, you are on track! The pain is good, and you'll want to bring up all these old memories; so you can realize that it's time to throw away all the garbage that's not doing anything for your life but stinking it up!

CONGRATULATIONS! You are coming out of denial, and into acknowledgment you are where you are right now in life due to all the choices you have made. You now realize there is no one to blame.

Remember coming out of denial is a huge step in the system, but once you get through it, acceptance will come much easier for you. It's just like riding a bike. The first few times riding, it's difficult. But after a while it becomes easy.

You are now reprogramming your mind! Excellent choice! You are now exercising your mind like you never have before. At first it will seem awkward and difficult. But in a short amount of time you will be able to operate your mind like you ride a bike.

Read this affirmation out loud with consistent, excited passion and desire!

"Right now I choose to take responsibility for all I have been blaming others for; I'm dumping the trash, on my way to an incredible, exciting, wonderful, abundant life I've always imagined."

CHAPTER SEVEN VIDEOS[6]

The links provided below, will bring you to a video visual summary of what you just read. It is a fun and quick demonstration, by me personally, to be used as a working tool and resource for your continued growth toward YOUR Victorious Mindset!

Denial, Part 1:
http://youtu.be/9ZP_78CdYWg

Denial, Part 2:
http://youtu.be/16X4MpXwI6k

Denial, Part 3:
http://youtu.be/6A5vsPUVuXI

---

[6]   "The author could have these videos remastered, but wanted to remain true to the realism of this initial training system and therefore, included videos as is. Some have slippage, but are still understandable. In the future, a remastered version will be available for purchase."

CHAPTER SEVEN PERSONAL NOTES SECTION FOR "DENIAL"

AUTHOR'S CHALLENGE

Read and consider the questions listed below and fill in your answers. This helps provide a working tool and resource for your continued growth toward YOUR Victorious Mindset!

1. My list of those I have blamed or have resentment against.

   a. _____

   b. _____

   c. _____

2. Below are my reasons why I blame them or have resentment towards them.

   a. _____

   b. _____

   c. _____

3. Below is the part I played in the above situations.

   a. _____

   b. _____

   c. _____

CHAPTER EIGHT

ACCEPTANCE

Acceptance: The act or process of accepting.

> Real problems are solvable,
> it's the imaginary obstacles
> that keep growing,
> so engage victory!
>
> Chip Esajian, Motivational Coach

STEP NUMBER THREE

You now choose to 'accept' your part in your pain! You choose to accept you make your own choices and accept the responsibility for the results of your decisions.

Remember you may not have had control over what was spoken into your life, or how you were physically treated. But you are responsible for thoughts you continue to hold on to. What's in the past is in the past.

Can you imagine what letting go of the pain from your past is going to do for you?

Now out of denial and no longer blaming anyone else for where you are in your life, it's time to accept it's ok! This is a huge victory for you, because all your actions have led you to this point where you have decided to change your life for the better.

You have already done the hard part of exposing the hidden burdens which weigh you down. Acceptance will come easier when you realize your past mistakes are no longer mistakes. You will now call them 'perfect experiences'!

Why? Because you want to verbalize to yourself in a positive way that you've learned from your past, it's not a 'screw up,' you're not an 'idiot,' it's a 'perfect experience'. Your Victorious Mindset will only develop when using positive reinforcement. You are now growing, stretching, and pushing yourself to create an entire new belief system.

Many people will say to themselves at this time, "If I had only done this long ago." That's the type of thinking you want to get rid of.

STOP going to the past, stop blaming yourself, this is only making you feel worse!

YOU ARE DONE TALKING TO YOURSELF LIKE YOU ARE A PIECE OF GARBAGE!

Accept all of your past shortcomings with a light sense of humor. Celebrate the fact you've come into acceptance of the part you played in your past.

I want to congratulate you on the courage you've shown to take these steps towards creating an extraordinary life of victory.

Read this affirmation out loud with consistent, excited passion and desire!

"Right now I take full responsibility for every choice I have made to this point, because I realize by taking responsibility and enjoying acceptance, I am setting myself free from blaming others. I am becoming a leader, and I have chosen to take control of my thoughts and create the life I've imagined! I am so excited about today's journey of the extraordinary life I have been given."

CHAPTER EIGHT VIDEOS[7]

The links provided below, will bring you to a video visual summary of what you just read. It is a fun and quick demonstration, by me personally, to be used as a working tool and resource for your continued growth toward YOUR Victorious Mindset!

Acceptance, Part 1:
http://youtu.be/KdRieXZG5nY

Acceptance, Part 2:
http://youtu.be/uFUr950oXng

---

[7] "The author could have these videos remastered, but wanted to remain true to the realism of this initial training system and therefore, included videos as is. Some have slippage, but are still understandable. In the future, a remastered version will be available for purchase."

Chapter Eight Personal Notes Section For "Acceptance"

_____

_____

_____

_____

_____

_____

_____

_____

_____

_____

_____

_____

_____

_____

_____

_____

_____

_____

_____

_____

_____

_____

_____

_____

_____

AUTHOR'S CHALLENGE

Read and consider the question listed below and fill in your answers. This helps provide a working tool and resource for your continued growth toward YOUR Victorious Mindset!

1. I accept and take responsibility for the following 'perfect experiences':

   a. _____

   _____

   b. _____

   _____

   c. _____

   _____

CHAPTER NINE

Forgiveness
The Key to Freedom

Forgiveness

Forgiveness: The act of forgiving; state of being forgiven.

As you better your
best, your
best becomes better!

Chip Esajian, Motivational Coach

Step Number Four

You now choose to 'forgive' all who have wronged you, ask 'forgiveness' of those you have wronged, and forgive yourself!

It is not always necessary to confront a person face-to-face to forgive them. Sometimes you can send a letter to the person or write the letter and mail it to yourself.

Or, you can pretend as if they are standing in front of you and practice the forgiveness process.

These are just a few ideas to get you started.

If you really want to begin to live, you have to forgive!

You've gotten out of denial, and you've acknowledged the part you played. Now it's time to forgive.

To forgive you have to let go of your pride and ego of being right.

So let's get you started on the fast track of the forgiveness process.

1. Focus on forgiving the offended person.
2. Focus on and look for the best quality in the offended person.
3. Focus on the qualities in the offended person, which attracted you to them in the first place because you used to like them.
4. Focus on loving them all over again.

What you focus on grows and expands, so by finding one good quality in the offended person and focusing in on it, you will begin to remember why you liked them in the first place. Isn't this what you would want someone to do if you had wronged them?

Practice this fast track forgiveness process until you have it mastered. Work all four of the steps listed above simultaneously with the goal of complete forgiveness.

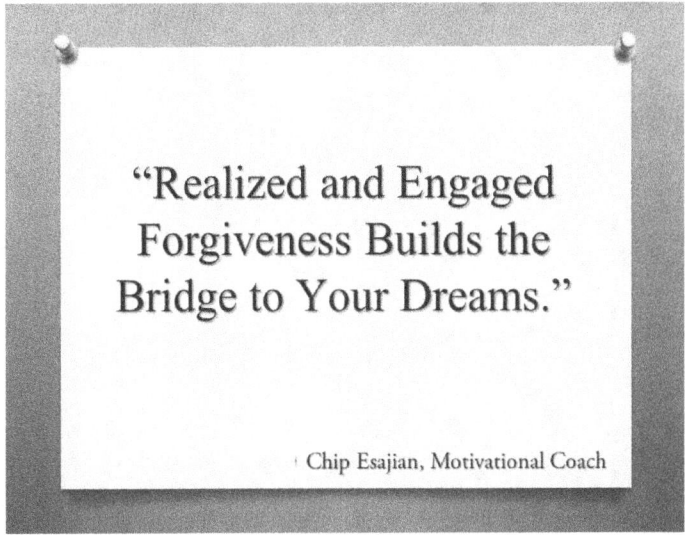

"Realized and Engaged Forgiveness Builds the Bridge to Your Dreams."

Chip Esajian, Motivational Coach

Why?

Because it clears your conscience and it takes you one step closer to building a victorious, abundant mindset. The goal is to see the offended person for who they could become again from a new perception you are now developing.

One less bitter thought about someone moves you one step closer to a victorious, abundant mindset. The goal is to have no enemies. As the bitterness decreases, so does the size of the mountains in front of your dreams.

Are you willing to let your ego and pride hold you back from an extraordinary happy life, where you love everyone, and have no enemies on your side of the street?

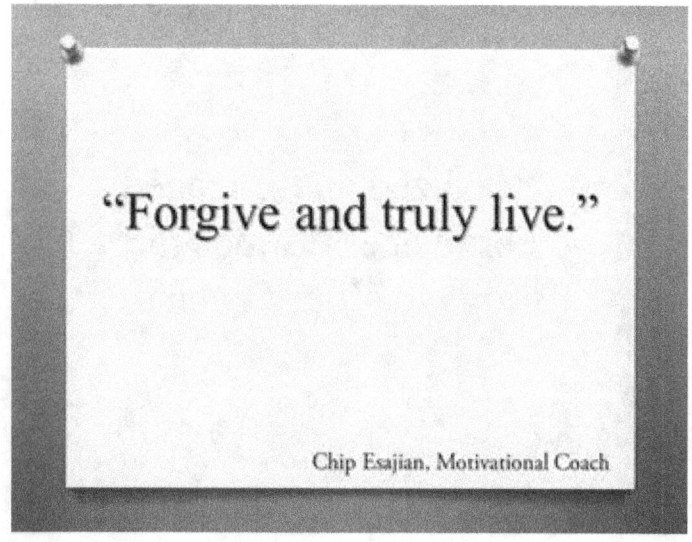

"Forgive and truly live."

Chip Esajian, Motivational Coach

You're going to have to practice the fast track forgiveness process if you want to change.

Imagine how much extra space there will be in your mind to create wonderful thoughts.

Remember, you are now working harder on your mind than you ever have! It's not used to being worked out in this fashion! So be courageous!

All the past unforgiveness, bitterness, and hate you have stored up has turned you into a person that is too annoying for extraordinary happiness to want to be around. By forgiving, you are removing the poison from your mind.

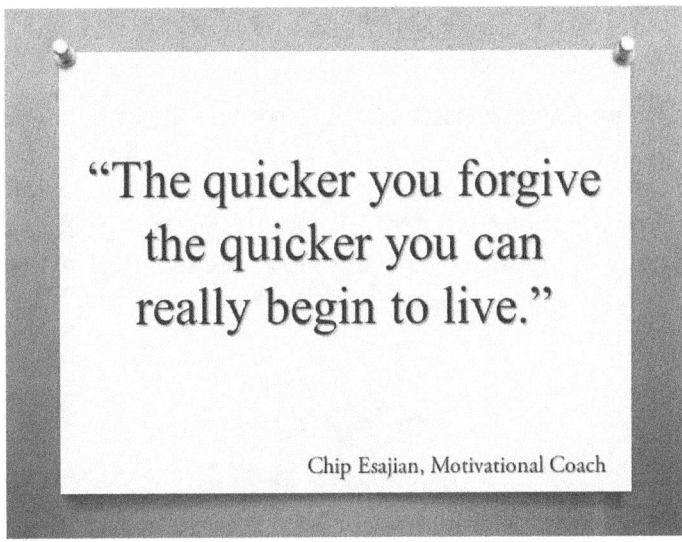

"The quicker you forgive the quicker you can really begin to live."

Chip Esajian, Motivational Coach

All you have to do is unhook those train cars from your "painful past closet" and let them drift away.

Let them go! Bye bye! Gone! Keep it simple!

You can do this! You are taking back control of your mind! **YOU** have climbed back in the control center of your brain and are reclaiming territory you didn't even know belonged to you! It's yours to command! You've been locked in sick bay as your star ship was on auto-pilot going around in circles.

Forgive yourself, forgive others, laugh at yourself, have a sense of humor, and open up the doors to freedom. There is an amazing place where you can float above your circumstances and create excited chills of happiness just from thinking about what an amazing life you have.

"Well Chip. I tried to forgive and it didn't work!"

This is where you need to practice. You will have to focus on forgiving the offended person. You are not forgiving them for their benefit. You are forgiving them for 'your' benefit.

Forgiving the person you have the most bitterness toward will be the toughest. But once you forgive them the rest will come easy. The excitement you receive from forgiving the offended person will fuel your passion to forgive others. It's then the dominos begin to fall. And, you become a master at forgiveness. Oh, how exciting this is!

Create amazing determination, and passion to forgive, because of the freedom you know you'll receive from doing it! Really practice and focus on letting go of the garbage that you have strapped to your back and have been carrying around with you everywhere you go. Now you should be starting to realize how poisonous bitterness and unforgiveness are to your life.

When you accomplish this step, you will have blown through a lot of the fear you used to hold on to.

Forgive and win, right now!

Forgiveness frees up a lot of space in your mind. Free your mind now!

Now isn't that an amazing feeling? We're just getting started!

CONGRATULATIONS ON COMPLETING THE FIRST FOUR STEPS! Congratulate yourself! Celebrate and focus on your wins every day!

Take time and focus on your wins, because they are the keys to taking back control of the command center of your brain!

Read this affirmation out loud with consistent, excited passion and desire!

"Right now I choose to forgive and let go of every negative thought for every person I am holding unforgiveness and negative thoughts against! Right now I'm going for happiness in my life that gives me chills! It starts with forgiveness, gratefulness, hope, and love!"

Chapter Nine Videos[8]

The links provided below, will bring you to a video visual summary of what you just read. It is a fun and quick demonstration, by me personally, to be used as a working tool and resource for your continued growth toward YOUR Victorious Mindset!

Forgiveness, Part 1:
http://youtu.be/vnJ6eeQ-OM0

Forgiveness, Part 2:
http://youtu.be/OLp0MQzijcM

Forgiveness, Part 3:
http://youtu.be/pZscZVsjgP4

---

8   "The author could have these videos remastered, but wanted to remain true to the realism of this initial training system and therefore, included videos as is. Some have slippage, but are still understandable. In the future, a remastered version will be available for purchase."

CHAPTER NINE PERSONAL NOTES SECTION FOR "FORGIVENESS"

_____

_____

_____

_____

_____

_____

_____

_____

_____

_____

_____

_____

_____

_____

_____

_____

_____

_____

_____

_____

_____

AUTHOR'S CHALLENGE

Read and consider the questions listed below and fill in your answers. This helps provide a working tool and resource for your continued growth toward YOUR Victorious Mindset!

1. Who do I need to forgive?

   a.

   b.

   c.

2. Who do I need to ask forgiveness from?

   a.

   b.

   c.

CHAPTER TEN

CAPTURE AND REPLACE
W/ BATTLE WORDS AND
PHRASES

Capture: To take by force, take prisoner and seize to gain control of or exert influence over.

Replace: To provide or to put one thing in place of another.

> Only the amazing power
> of forgiveness can fill
> the consuming hunger of
> hate and bitterness!
>
> Chip Esajian, Motivational Coach

Step Number Five

Y ou now choose to 'capture' and 'replace' your thought-life vocabulary. Replace the old hard drive with a new one. Choose to replace old negative thoughts with new, positive, exciting, powerful, wonderful, abundant, and extraordinary thoughts!

Now that you have gone through and completed Steps 1 through 4, you may realize your brain is not your friend. And, it does not want you to be its master. Consider you have been your mind's slave. Your brain has been on auto pilot. It's time to take back control of your thoughts. It's time to climb back into the command center of your brain and take back control of your life!

Your brain is where a belief turns into a thought, which turns into an attitude, into an emotion, into behavior, into words, and into actions which are all controlled by your belief system. You are on your way to building an unlimited belief system where all things are possible.

One thing to always remember, your brain runs your heart, not vice versa. A thought produces an emotion. Think about this, when you have different thoughts throughout a day; those thoughts produce emotions whether they are good or bad.

You have built habitual, negative, limited beliefs which form your thoughts. Your thoughts are a movie reel playing on auto pilot 24 hours a day in your mind. This is a reflection of who you think you are; which affects your view of others.

Now you're ready to capture and replace all of your negative thoughts, with new wonderful, positive, loving, exciting, beautiful, and extraordinary thoughts!

It's very simple, every negative thought you have about yourself, another person, place, or thing is to be immediately countered by a victoriously affirmative thought. This is to be done all throughout your day, every time you have a negative thought.

Now remember, to have extraordinary victories, you have to go through extraordinary battles courageously. Capturing and replacing your thoughts will take extreme energy, focus, and practice to get good at. But the rewards are priceless.

Below I will demonstrate a few examples of how to capture a thought and, what to replace it with. The first sentence is a thought you might say to yourself that you will *capture* the moment you find yourself thinking it.

The second sentence is a sample of what to *replace* it with.

'This day sucks.'
'**This day is wonderful**.'

'I hate my job, is it Friday yet?'
'**I'm so grateful for the opportunity to work here, I'm making it the most incredible opportunity of my life, and every day is Saturday.**'

'My life is terrible and going nowhere.'
'**My life is wonderful, and something wonderful is happening to me today**.'

There are more examples of replacement words and phrases at the end of this chapter to show how simple the process is. Again, it takes practice and here's the process you'll go through.

First, you'll have a negative thought that will *trigger* you to counter the negative thought with a positive thought. Repeat that positive thought several times! With continued practice, daily, the distance between a *captured* negative thought and a *replaced* positive thought will get shorter. A negative thought will trigger you straight into a positive thought. With daily repetition, your negative thoughts will start to disappear, and be replaced with more positive thoughts.

Capture negative thoughts and replace them with incredible, exciting, wonderful thoughts!

STAY FOCUSED! Work on your new exciting Victorious Mindset daily. Work on this harder than you've ever worked on anything else, and your rewards will be nothing short of extraordinary!

At first it will be hard, and you will experience a lot of frustration, but if you are courageous, passionate, consistent, disciplined, and committed, you will begin to have a lot of fun and success with the process. Stay committed and do not quit once you start creating your Victorious Mindset.

For example, can you imagine a doctor stopping half way through an operation or a mechanic stopping half way through putting a new engine in a car? That would be ridiculous, but it is exactly what you would be doing by giving up halfway through the process.

Read this affirmation out loud with consistent, excited passion and desire!

"Today, I choose to capture all my negative thoughts and replace them with happy, exciting, wonderful, abundant, and extraordinary thoughts, and will settle for nothing less than amazing success."

Replacement Battle Words and Phrases

Now here are a few examples of capturing and replacing your thoughts. You can add more as you experience different negative thoughts.

I'm not special
I'm a miracle

I can't
I can

Life is terrible
Life is wonderful

What an idiot mistake I made
It's a perfect experience

I'm ugly
I'm beautiful

I'm sad
I'm happy

I'm stupid
I'm smart

This is impossible
All things are possible

I'm not important
I was created for extraordinary

Why _____ ?
I'm working toward a solution

I'm bored
I'm going to create some excitement

I'm discouraged
I'm excited about encouraging myself

I'm tired
I'm energized

I'm not good enough
I'm unique and have a wonderful purpose

It's not my fault
I take full responsibility

I'm miserable
I'm creating happiness from gratefulness

Life's not fair
Life is fair and full of opportunities

I'm not forgiving them
I forgive them and let go of the burden

I'm afraid
I'm courageous

They're idiots
They have amazing potential

Your goal is to capture all your limited beliefs and negative thoughts. Then replace them with unlimited beliefs, extraordinary positive thoughts about yourself, others, and every situation in your life.

CHAPTER TEN VIDEOS[9]

The links provided below, will bring you to a video visual summary of what you just read. It is a fun and quick demonstration, by me personally, to be used as a working tool and resource for your continued growth toward YOUR Victorious Mindset!

Capture & Replace Your Thoughts, Part 1:
http://youtu.be/Tp6Jxc5WcyI

Capture & Replace Your Thoughts, Part 2:
http://youtu.be/L3iRXzgjW5w

Capture & Replace Your Thoughts, Part 3:
http://youtu.be/j23xA8ggdCs

---

[9] The author could have these videos remastered, but wanted to remain true to the realism of this initial training system and therefore, included videos as is. Some have slippage, but are still understandable. In the future, a remastered version will be available for purchase."

CHAPTER TEN PERSONAL NOTES SECTION FOR "CAPTURE AND REPLACE YOUR THOUGHTS"

_____

_____

_____

_____

_____

_____

_____

_____

_____

_____

_____

_____

_____

_____

_____

_____

AUTHOR'S CHALLENGE

It's time for you to make your list of 'capture' and 'replacement' words and phrases, which will assist you on a day-to-day basis.

My top ten:

NEGATIVE THOUGHTS I NEED TO CAPTURE	VICTORIOUS REPLACEMENT THOUGHTS
1	1
2	2
3	3
4	4
5	5
6	6
7	7
8	8
9	9
10	10

CHAPTER ELEVEN

Practice

Practice: Repeated performance or systematic exercise for the purpose of acquiring skill or proficiency.

If you
WANT BETTER
THINK BETTER!

Chip Esajian, Motivational Coach

STEP NUMBER SIX

Y ou now choose to 'practice' your new thought life with belief and persistence 24 hours a day, 7 days a week! Practice is the key to becoming great at anything you do in life! You can learn anything, but it is the practice, which perfects what you've learned!

If you practice repeating the phrase, 'Something wonderful is happening to me today,' and 'My life is wonderful' 100 to 200 times per day (to replace negative thoughts), do you think you might begin to believe it? How fast do you want to start having wonderful days? If you're not practicing having wonderful days, then you're practicing having negative, self-destructive days! Hmm ... let's see ... this should be a no brainer choice for you.

You can take a karate lesson and learn a move, but if you don't practice the move, you have accomplished nothing.

PRACTICE positive choices, **PRACTICE** getting out of denial, **PRACTICE** acceptance, **PRACTICE** forgiveness, **PRACTICE** capturing and replacing, **PRACTICE, PRACTICE, PRACTICE, PRACTICE, PRACTICE, PRACTICE**!

Remember, *The Victorious Mindset* is your around the clock training system manual! If you practice victorious, wonderful, exciting thoughts, then you will develop a habit of creating victorious happiness in your life to overflow onto others.

From the time you wake up to the time you go to sleep, you need to practice capturing and replacing your thoughts! The more you practice the better you get. Either you will want to fly like an eagle every day, or crawl like a turtle!

The **CHOICE** is up to **YOU**!

Read this affirmation out loud with consistent, excited passion and desire!

"Right now I'm practicing a wonderful thought life. I'm practicing grateful, thankful, exciting, loving, wonderful, giving, extraordinary, abundant thoughts,

which have nothing to do with the circumstances that I am floating above."

> "If you want to get better at better thinking, practice thinking better thoughts and you'll get better at better thinking!"
>
> Chip Esajian, Motivational Coach

CHAPTER ELEVEN VIDEOS[10]

The link provided below, will bring you to a video visual summary of what you just read. It is a fun and quick demonstration, by me personally, to be used as a working tool and resource for your continued growth toward YOUR Victorious Mindset!

http://youtu.be/1uqoUSeN0qQ

---

[10] " The author could have these videos remastered, but wanted to remain true to the realism of this initial training system and therefore, included videos as is. Some have slippage, but are still understandable. In the future, a remastered version will be available for purchase."

CHAPTER ELEVEN PERSONAL NOTES SECTION "PRACTICE"

_____

_____

_____

_____

_____

_____

_____

_____

_____

_____

_____

_____

_____

_____

_____

_____

_____

_____

_____

_____

_____

_____

AUTHOR'S CHALLENGE

Read and consider the questions listed below and fill in your answers. This helps provide a working tool and resource for your continued growth toward YOUR Victorious Mindset!

1. What new thought processes are you committing to practice to get better at better thinking?

2. When are the times throughout your day you can practice?
   a) When negative thoughts first come to mind.
   b) When I don't have to think about what I'm doing: washing dishes, eating, getting ready for work, when I am driving, etc.

   c)

   d)

   e)

CHAPTER TWELVE

BECOME

Become: To grow or come to be.

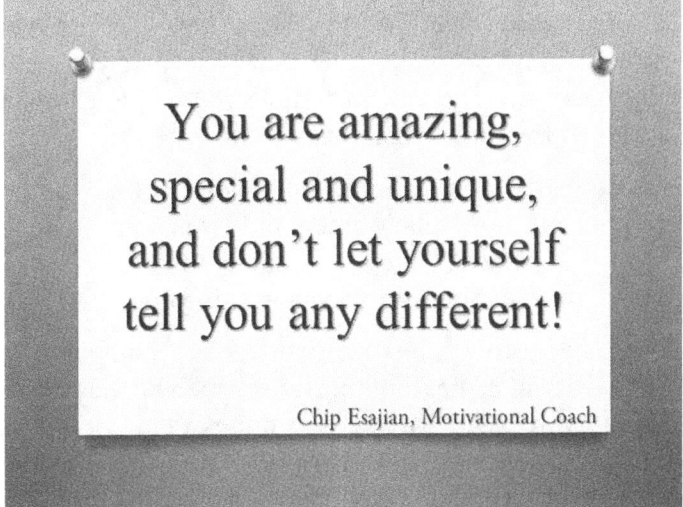

You are amazing,
special and unique,
and don't let yourself
tell you any different!

Chip Esajian, Motivational Coach

STEP NUMBER SEVEN

Choose to 'become' what you practice! Forgiveness, inspiration, etc. What you focus on expands, and that you become.

Welcome to becoming what you have been practicing in Steps 1-6. Congratulations on creating your new Victorious Mindset!

You have been practicing your Victorious Mindset and now you are becoming what you have practiced! You are becoming victorious and happy. You have taken back control of the command center of your brain and you are learning to turn on the victory and abundance at all times. That is what Step 7 "Become" is all about.

You are now taking charge of your life, and becoming incredibly valuable to yourself and soon to others around you. Not only are you changing who you are but also how you see the world. Take time to embrace who you are now becoming, the new you, that you never knew existed. The new incredible you will touch many people's lives in amazing ways.

If you had a friend who talked to you the way you talk to yourself, how much time would you want to spend with that person? Now you should be getting excited about your relationship you have with yourself.

You are starting to realize richness and abundance are built within. It has nothing to do with money or the things you have! Money and things don't bring true happiness. Becoming the miracle that God created you to be is beginning to bring that happiness.

You should now be starting to realize that you are not here on earth for just yourself, but you are here to make a difference in other people's lives!

Practice something enough and you begin to become extraordinary at what you have practiced!

To excel faster to whom you want to become, continue to practice 24 hours a day, 7 days a week, nonstop!

Read this affirmation out loud with consistent, excited passion and desire!

"Right now, today, I am becoming a grateful, thankful, happy, excited, and abundant new me that I am excited to be around! I'm happy, healthy, wealthy, excited, congruent, confident, and victorious! PBG is practicing, becoming, and giving."

CHAPTER TWELVE VIDEOS[11]

The link provided below, will bring you to a video visual summary of what you just read. It is a fun and quick demonstration, by me personally, to be used as a working tool and resource for your continued growth toward YOUR Victorious Mindset!

http://youtu.be/0TvmCoWaPdk

---

[11] "The author could have these videos remastered, but wanted to remain true to the realism of this initial training system and therefore, included videos as is. Some have slippage, but are still understandable. In the future, a remastered version will be available for purchase."

CHAPTER TWELVE PERSONAL NOTES
SECTION "BECOME"

_____

_____

_____

_____

_____

_____

_____

_____

_____

_____

_____

_____

_____

_____

_____

_____

_____

_____

_____

_____

_____

_____

_____

AUTHOR'S CHALLENGE

Read and consider the questions listed below and fill in your answers as a resource for your continued growth toward YOUR Victorious Mindset!

1. What kind of person do you want to become?
   a.

   b.

   c.

2. How would this type of person think and behave?
   a.

   b.

   c.

"When you always practice to become more than you are, you will consistently grow to become more than you were!"

Chip Esajian, Motivational Coach

CHAPTER THIRTEEN

give

Give: To present voluntarily and without expecting compensation; to bestow.

> If you want happiness,
> notify your mind
> you're taking control,
> then create wonderful
> thoughts.
>
> Chip Esajian, Motivational Coach

step number eight

Choose to now 'give' what you've practiced and become! Giving is living! Now you are building the habit of practicing a Victorious Mindset, you are becoming that which you've practiced. Once you've practiced something so much, with determined focus, belief, passion, and a strategy for success, you become that thing! You can now give it away effortlessly!

PRACTICE FORGIVENESS enough every day and you will become excellent at it. You will become forgiveness and then you will be able to give it. If you want to become inspirational, you have to practice inspiration. Practice inspiration enough, and you will become inspiration and then you will automatically give it away to others everyday effortlessly.

A secret to true happiness is giving. But to be able to give unconditionally we have to create an extraordinary Victorious Mindset that will overflow onto others. When you are overflowing with happiness, gratefulness, thankfulness, and excitement for life, others will want what you have. You will love giving it away!

You are now beginning to understand that one of the most important secrets in life to happiness is cleaning up our own side of the street, so that we can see others on it! Only then when you have let go of the old life of the selfish stinking thinking you had, will you be able to look up high enough to see a new world that exists, that you have opened up, by choosing a higher standard for your life.

By choosing a higher standard for your life, others will now begin to view your life as a higher standard that they will want to live by. Why? Because there is so much happiness, peace, excitement, love, caring, fulfillment, and purpose in you! You are now becoming a leader of men/women. You have jumped into the top 3% of the population of the world that wants extraordinary happiness and abundance in their lives, and are doing something about it!!

To give unconditionally you must stop expecting a certain response, from others, for you to be happy.

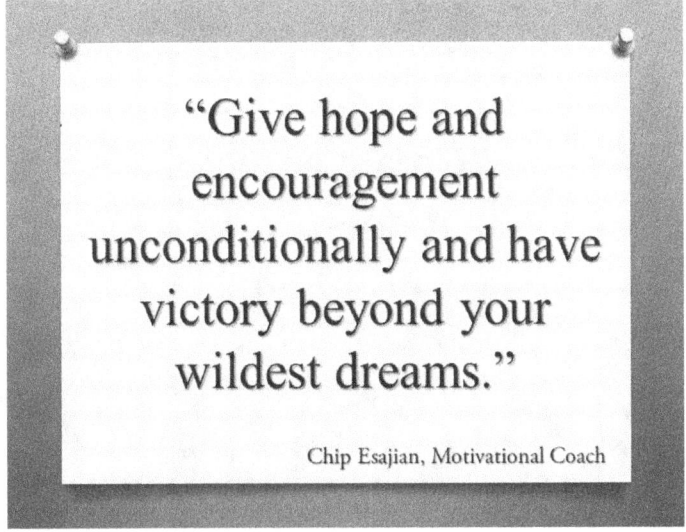

"Give hope and encouragement unconditionally and have victory beyond your wildest dreams."

Chip Esajian, Motivational Coach

One of my friends mentioned to me that she gets so frustrated with people, when she tells them that 'life is wonderful' and 'have a great day' and they moan and groan back. So she tells them 'have a great day' anyway, but still walks away frustrated. The key word she used in that sentence was 'frustrated.'

Did she win or lose? Now think about that for a moment. You start out your morning all excited! You are fired up and the first person you run into, you greet with an exciting, 'Hey my friend, extraordinary day to you,' and they respond with, 'yeah right.'

You end up thinking about that the whole day. You didn't get the response you wanted from a person you had no control over, you got frustrated and let it ruin your day.

Not only did you get frustrated, but you dwelled on that person negatively all throughout your day. That my friend is insanity, yet we have all done it for most of our lives every single day! Now that is funny.

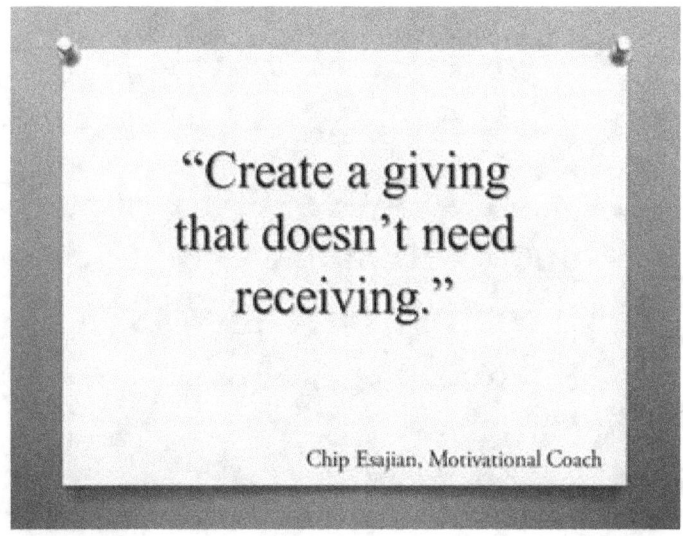

"Create a giving that doesn't need receiving."

Chip Esajian, Motivational Coach

It's simple. Do not worry about how someone else will respond to your kindness or encouragement. We as people set ourselves up every single crazy day by expecting others to respond to us a certain way. When they don't we let it ruin our day! Why? Because we have a false sense of expectation about how someone should respond to us.

Think about it, everyone does it with almost every human encounter. I'm laughing right now just writing this! I was so excited about this discovery in my life. People do not know how to respond to me when I say, "You were created for extraordinary my friend, and there's no one that looks like you! You have an amazing purpose!" How many times have you had someone come up and say that to you? Or I'll say to someone, "Make it an extraordinary wonderful day my friend," and they have this bewildered look on their face as they retort 'sure . . . you too.'

Keep moving through your day. Keep momentum on your side with your Victorious Mindset! Prepare for victory with others before it happens. If people do respond with a response you love, you appreciate it even more.

Give what you've practiced and become to others without expecting a certain answer from them. You are building a confidence in your life that will not need other people's stamp of approval on it.

You have practiced your Victorious Mindset! You are becoming victorious! You are giving victory!

Read this affirmation out loud with consistent, excited passion and desire!

> *"I am victorious in practicing, becoming, and now giving to others the victorious abundance that I've created in my life without thought of receiving, but of capturing the true fulfillment of pure giving."*

CHAPTER THIRTEEN VIDEOS[12]

The link provided below, will bring you to a video visual summary of what you just read. It is a fun and quick demonstration, by me personally, to be used as a working tool and resource for your continued growth toward YOUR Victorious Mindset!

http://youtu.be/iKT009k7AJQ

---

[12] "The author could have these videos remastered, but wanted to remain true to the realism of this initial training system and therefore, included videos as is. Some have slippage, but are still understandable. In the future, a remastered version will be available for purchase."

CHAPTER THIRTEEN PERSONAL NOTES
SECTION "GIVE"

_____

_____

_____

_____

_____

_____

_____

_____

_____

_____

_____

_____

_____

_____

_____

_____

_____

_____

_____

_____

_____

_____

_____

AUTHOR'S CHALLENGE

Read and consider the questions listed below and fill in your answers. This helps provide a working tool and resource for your continued growth toward YOUR Victorious Mindset!

1. What would you like to be able to give effortlessly to others?

   a.

   b.

   c.

2. In what ways could you give to others each day?

   a.

   b.

   c.

CHAPTER FOURTEEN

Dream

Dream: A goal or aim; something of unreal beauty.

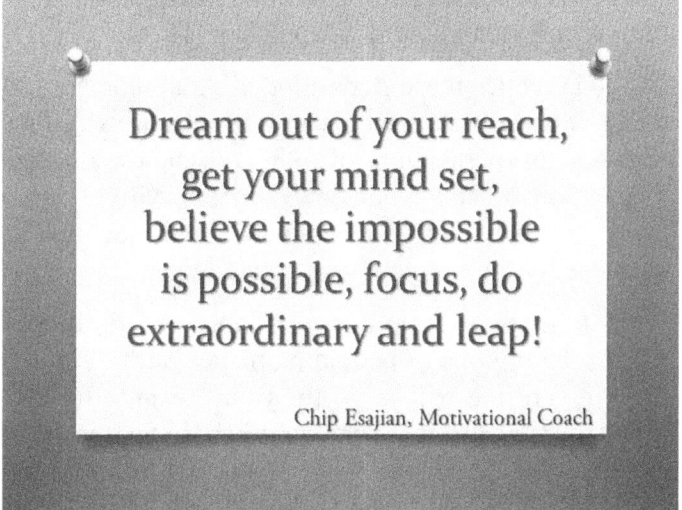

> Dream out of your reach,
> get your mind set,
> believe the impossible
> is possible, focus, do
> extraordinary and leap!
>
> Chip Esajian, Motivational Coach

Step Number Nine

Choose to realize your 'dream,' which has emerged from working the first eight steps of "The Victorious Mindset Training System."

CONGRATULATIONS!

You are now at the point in your battle training, where your imagination may be opening up for the first time in your life, in a way you never believed possible!

Prior to beginning battle training with *The Victorious Mindset*, your mind was working you and dragging you behind it as it had its way with you. Reality is, you chose to have your mind on auto pilot for all the days of your life up to this point. Now you can say, "Enough is enough," and make a new choice to climb back into the command center of your mind and take control!

The greatest asset you were created with is your mind. You have the ability to take captive every thought and turn it into victory towards abundance!

As you practice these steps a lot of 'Aha' moments take place. You begin to see the world in an entirely different way. Your perception of others changes and your perception of how you view yourself will change as well. In time, you will begin to see the dreams and purpose for the life you were created for.

Remember there is no one who looks exactly like you out of the billions of people on planet earth! You have been given free will to go for your dreams. But along life's journey, through your years here so far, the limited beliefs you developed as a 'fact of life' may have overtook you and blinded your view of what was possible for you! Then somewhere along the way your inner passion to be more than you are, pushed its way through your limited beliefs, to believe that you can be more than you are!

Your dreams are what set you apart from everyone else! They're your dreams. Yet, your dreams will take different shapes as you grow in your Victorious Mindset of abundance. As you grow and work on your mind, harder than you work on anything else, you will begin to see a world of peace, joy, happiness, excitement, etc. You will be so overflowing with these feelings, emotions, and gifts that you will want to give them to others to enrich their lives!

A great man once said: If you help enough people fulfill their dreams, you will be standing in your own. And, the Bible says it perfectly: "Give, and it will be given to you. A good measure, pressed down, shaken together and running over, will be poured into your lap."[13]

Now, it's time to dream big!

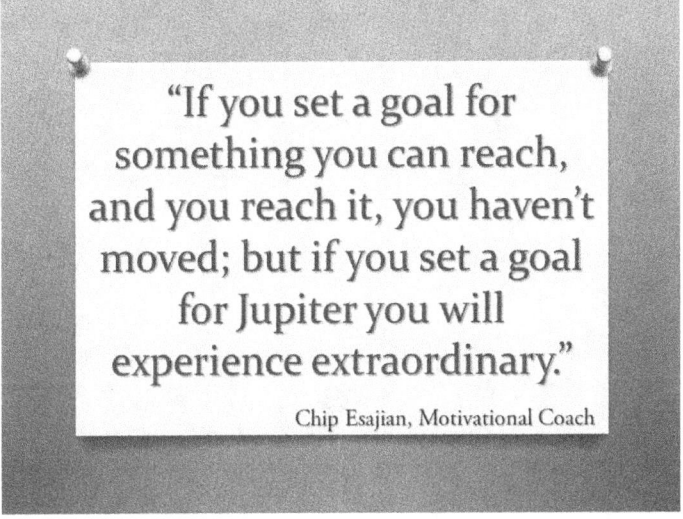

> "If you set a goal for something you can reach, and you reach it, you haven't moved; but if you set a goal for Jupiter you will experience extraordinary."
>
> Chip Esajian, Motivational Coach

Go for extraordinary and dream so big you have no idea how you're going to get there. You know you will, because of the new unlimited beliefs you are developing every day! The "how" doesn't matter! What matters is that you see the end result and build the bridge to it! You have to know where you want to go, or you will wander in the wilderness aimlessly!

---

[13] Luke 6:38 (NIV).

The key is to enjoy and be excited on the journey! Enjoying the journey is what makes getting there so breathtaking!

Read this affirmation out loud with consistent, excited passion and desire!

"Today, I'm courageous, grateful and thankful, I engage my mindset and believe the impossible to be possible and fly."

CHAPTER FOURTEEN VIDEOS[14]

The links provided below, will bring you to a video visual summary of what you just read. It is a fun and quick demonstration, by me personally, to be used as a working tool and resource for your continued growth toward YOUR Victorious Mindset!

Dream, Part 1:
http://youtu.be/xuwa_nSJbsY

Dream, Part 2:
http://youtu.be/YZNzTX2qk18

Dream, Part 3:
http://youtu.be/ziEPTpNx4hc

---

[14] "The author could have these videos remastered, but wanted to remain true to the realism of this initial training system and therefore, included videos as is. Some have slippage, but are still understandable. In the future, a remastered version will be available for purchase."

Chapter Fourteen Personal Notes Section "Dream"

_____

_____

_____

_____

_____

_____

_____

_____

_____

_____

_____

_____

_____

_____

_____

_____

_____

_____

_____

AUTHOR'S CHALLENGE

Read and consider the questions listed below and fill in your answers. This helps provide a working tool and resource for your continued growth toward YOUR Victorious Mindset!

1. What are a couple of dreams you have for your future?

   a.

   b.

   c.

2. On a scale from 1 to 10, 10 being the highest, how committed are you to creating the Victorious Mindset you'll need to reach your dream?

   a.

   b.

   c.

HOW HIGH
DO YOU WANT TO FLY?

Circle One

10

9

8

7

6

5

4

3

2

1

CHAPTER FIFTEEN

OTHERS

Others: Other persons or other people.

NO GRATITUDE
NO VICTORY

~

HAVE GRATITUDE
HAVE VICTORY

Chip Esajian, Motivational Coach

STEP NUMBER TEN

Y ou choose to realize the amazing abundant life you've created will be realized, by helping 'others' fulfill their dreams in all areas of their lives!

You need others to win in life. No one is an island. The most wonderful feeling in the world is having an extraordinary mindset of victory, gratefulness, and happiness to overflow onto others. When you are excited about life, others see it. When you are depressed and complaining about everything and everybody, others hear it. That is the impression you leave on their mind. Therefore, if you give victorious abundance to people on a consistent basis, it is what they will remember you for and be inspired by and they will most likely look forward to seeing you again.

If you give others a victim mentality mindset, it is what people will remember you for. They will most likely not want to be around you again in the future because it brings them down. Create what people will remember and be inspired by. Be extraordinary.

The first nine steps set it all up for you! Your dreams and purpose are unfolding before you as you create your Victorious Mindset. Your dreams and purpose should include taking others with you along the way. By now, you see life in a different way. By now, you are looking for people to encourage and share your new Victorious Mindset with! For example, if you see an amazing movie, you can't wait to tell people about it. If something amazing is happening in your life, you tell everyone around you about it. When you create a Victorious Mindset of extraordinary abundance and your life begins to change, believe me you are going to tell everyone around!

You will have a new energy to become a contagious virus of victorious happiness, which will overflow from you onto others! And that, my friend, is what you were created for; to give others hope and encouragement that there is an amazing life they were created for!

EVERYONE NEEDS HOPE! Everyone has a dream, even if they say they don't. They just can't see it yet because of all the garbage that has them stuffed in the back of their 'painful past closet.' You should now be starting to realize when you give hope and encouragement you are lifting others higher than they've ever been before. I'll say it again, when you create a wonderful life others can see incredible value in, they will want what you have!

Everyone wants a dream, hope, encouragement, peace, love, passion, happiness, abundance, and purpose! So if you create and possess these attributes, you are valuable to that person!

There is a great verse in the Bible: *"Where there is no vision the people perish..."*[15] This statement is so incredibly true. If you have no purpose for living what is life worth living for?

Have you ever felt pressured by the world around you, that you were just not quite what you should be? Well, our success-driven society makes it easy to believe that lie. I realized it's not about "he with the most toys wins", because I have never been to a funeral and seen a U-Haul attached to a hearse. I have never seen anyone trying to stick a 50 inch flat screen TV in the grave with the person. Since those are plain facts, then life has to have a much larger purpose. **OH YEAH!** Since you were born naked, and you are going out of this world naked, life is about something else!

It's about others! What you sow, you reap. If you want extraordinary in your life, then give extraordinary to

---

[15]   Prov. 29:18 (KJV)

others. Well, these 10 steps are the beginning of an incredible journey you have begun!

Remember, if you want to be inspirational, you have to "Practice" (Step 6) inspiration. Then with enough practice you will "Become" (Step 7) what you've practiced. Then once you've practiced and become inspiration, you will automatically "Give" (Step 8) it to others; because you are so full of excitement from creating your new Victorious Mindset, that your passion will overtake you and others will want to be around you!

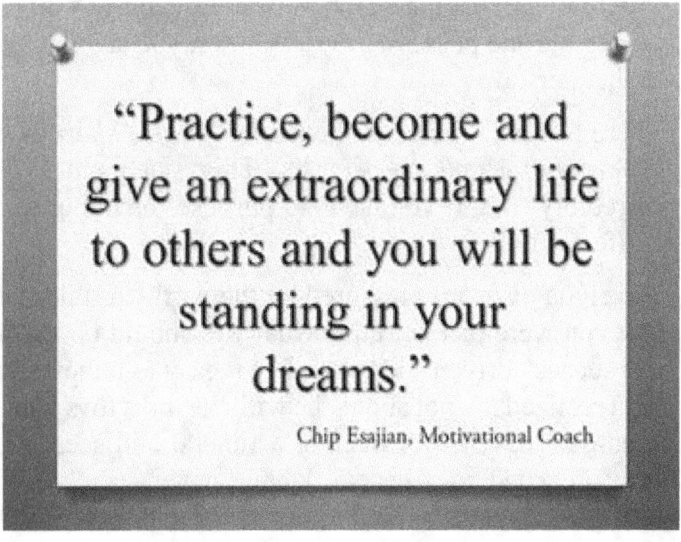

"Practice, become and give an extraordinary life to others and you will be standing in your dreams."

Chip Esajian, Motivational Coach

How many people want to be around a complainer? How many people want to be around someone who is whining all the time?

Everyone loves encouragement! Everyone loves to feel special! Everyone wants to believe that they have an important purpose! Everyone loves to feel needed! Everyone would love to be truly happy!

The world is dysfunctional, and everyone needs victory in their life. They have dreamed about happiness all their lives and thought that it's a place you arrive at when you've made enough money! People think the grass is always greener on the other side of the fence. What they don't realize is that the guy that lives next to them is saying the same thing. Billions of people are looking for that abundant life they've always imagined, but have no clue how to get there, or what it really is. It's always been an 'out of reach' idea hasn't it? And sorry folks, but going to college, getting a degree, going into the military, or getting a certain job doesn't teach you the simple system you're learning in *The Victorious Mindset*!

You are working on your brain to work for you! This book is giving you the extraordinary skills that, if applied to your life with passionate consistent practice, will open up an amazing world of incredible opportunities! You will completely change your life, and the lives of everyone else you come in contact with!

Once you begin creating your Victorious Mindset, it never ends. Yes, creating your Victorious Mindset will take a lot of focus and determination; however, I have found that it becomes real easy and automatic to do after a while. So, as I said before, what else are you doing here on planet earth anyway? You might as well bring heaven to earth while you're at it, and give it to as many people as possible.

You are learning that true fulfillment comes when you create meaning in others' lives, beyond what they've ever experienced.

Instead of being just a good friend, be an extraordinary friend. Be such an amazing friend to other people that they want to raise their standards of living to the same abundant life you are experiencing! Without others you are alone.

Congratulations on Completing Your Ten Steps to Victorious Abundance!

You have now begun the exciting journey to find your true purpose, of what it is you were created for. Do you think it's all by accident you have become sick and tired of being sick and tired, of putting up with yourself enough to now do something about it? Of course not! The timing is perfect for you to go for extraordinary in your life!

You picked up this training system and have made one of the greatest choices of your life! You were created for **EXTRAORDINARY**! There is no one who looks like you; you are unique, special, and you have been given a dream that is now beginning to emerge, that was meant for you to reach. Now you have been given the tools to be able to see that dream! And not only to see that dream, but to surpass it!

Congratulations my extraordinary friend!

CHaPter FiFteen VideoS[16]

The links provided below, will bring you to a video visual summary of what you just read. It is a fun and quick demonstration, by me personally, to be used as a working tool and resource for your continued growth toward YOUR Victorious Mindset!

Others, Part 1:
http://youtu.be/wGE1cgZqnk8

Others, Part 2:
http://youtu.be/zITGFdfR-D8

Others, Part 3:
http://youtu.be/yrMOEWFPzTQ

---

[16] The author could have these videos remastered, but wanted to remain true to the realism of this initial training system and therefore, included videos as is. Some have slippage, but are still understandable. In the future, a remastered version will be available for purchase."

CHAPTER FIFTEEN PERSONAL NOTES
SECTION "OTHERS"

AUTHOR'S CHALLENGE

When you have completed your list below, make the effort to 'give' to these people, through encouragement, each time you see them. Pay attention to what they talk about and support their interests, thank them for their friendship, let them know you appreciate their humor, complement their talents, when they're feeling down tell them they WILL find a way to bounce back, etc.

1. Make a list of ten people in your everyday life that you could encourage:

1. _____

2. _____

3. _____

4. _____

5. _____

6. _____

7. _____

8. _____

9. _____

10. _____

encouragements

1.   Victorious day to you!
2.   Your future is incredibly bright!
3.   Your most wonderful moments are ahead of you!
4.   You were created for extraordinary!
5.   I'm so happy to see you today!
6.
7.
8.
9.
10.
11.
12.
13.
14.
15.
16.
17.
18.
19.
20.

CHAPTER SIXTEEN
THE FOUR QUESTIONS TO ALWAYS ASK YOURSELF

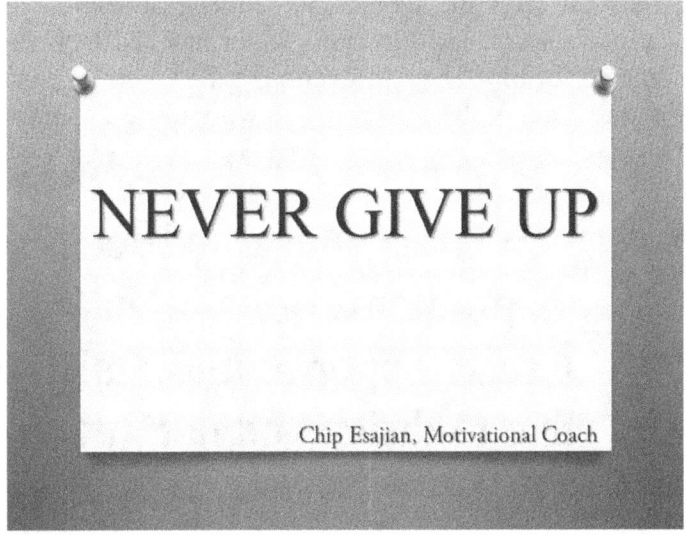

NEVER GIVE UP

Chip Esajian, Motivational Coach

WHEN FACED WITH CHALLENGES!

1. What is the worst case scenario?
2. What is the most realistic scenario?
3. What is the best case scenario?
4. What is the scenario I will create regardless of the other 3?

By asking yourself these four questions every time you run into obstacles, you are moving towards solution! You are shifting your mind into proactive, solution-creating mode!

Get past the fate of the worst case scenario, by really engaging, and paper trailing what is the cause and effect of the worst that can happen. Then really examine that scenario until you take the emotion out of it. Do that with all the scenarios, and use it in your everyday life! Get real with the worst, most likely, and best case scenario's with each situation you experience upon your journey in life. Then you can take the emotion, panic, and fear out of the equation, and work toward solution!

> "What is your mind set on, problems or solutions? Create opportunities and live to thrive and not just survive."
>
> Chip Esajian, Motivational Coach

CHAPTER SIXTEEN PERSONAL NOTES SECTION "THE 4 QUESTIONS TO ALWAYS ASK YOURSELF"

AUTHOR'S CHALLENGE

Read and consider the questions listed below and fill in your answers. This helps provide a working tool and resource for your continued growth toward YOUR Victorious Mindset!

1. What is the most recent obstacle or circumstance in your life to take emotion out of, so you can work toward a solution?

    a.

    b.

    c.

2. What is the worst case scenario?

    a.

    b.

    c.

3. What is the most realistic scenario?

    a.

    b.

    c.

4. What is the best case scenario?

    a.

    b.

c.

5. What is the scenario you will create regardless of the other 3?

a.

b.

c.

CHAPTER SEVENTEEN

THE DAILY POWER START AND MAINTENANCE SYSTEM

> If you want
> to change
> another's view,
> change you!
>
> Chip Esajian, Motivational Coach

Your 'morning power start' is the most important time of the day! From the minute your head leaves your pillow you must shift your mind into victorious power mode.

To do this, I use my "Daily Power Start and Maintenance System" the first 15 to 30 minutes of every day! Then I use only part of it throughout the rest of my day to power up and maintain my Victorious Mindset. Set yourself up to win by having everything set up the night before, so it will be ready for you first thing the next morning.

"Set yourself up for success every moment of every day with extraordinary victorious power."

Chip Esajian, Motivational Coach

DAILY POWER

Start System

There are six 'Phases' to follow. I would suggest you either: write out each one on a sheet of paper, type it up to print out, or write it in this book. The goal is to be able to have this information with you, wherever you go, every day! These lists should be updated and added too, as you feel it's necessary: weekly, bi-monthly, monthly. They will grow in length and change as you grow and change through using "The Victorious Mindset Training System."

Phase one

Write down 20 to 50 or more things you are grateful for. The first few things might include: your heart is beating, you're breathing involuntarily, or you can see the words you are reading and so forth.

Get grateful for the small things, such as being able to move your fingers. You can think about your fingers moving and they move. That, my friend, is a miracle!

'Power Start' every morning by reading this list you've completed, out loud, and then rereading this list at least 2 more times throughout your day as 'Maintenance.' I'm grateful for…

1.

2.

3.

4.

5.

6.

7.

8.

9.

10.

11.

12.

13.

14.

15.

16.

17.

18.

19.

20.

PHASE TWO

Exciting things in life are inspiring, cause us to move forward, give us energy. An example of what excited me as I wrote this book was: I'm excited about getting closer to paying-off my debts, getting better at my job each day - which benefits my company and myself, being a better husband for my wonderful wife, battling through the hard times right now expecting the victory soon! Now it's your turn to put it in writing.

What am I excited about or want to be excited about?

1.

2.

3.

Pha/e Three

Quotes are used to stretch your mind to think beyond your current level of understanding and/or thinking. Page ahead to Chapter 20 and pick out 5 quotes that are 'meaningful' to you, which you will say aloud to 'Start' each morning. Then pick one of the 5 quotes to focus on specifically throughout each day as 'Maintenance' for 1 to 2 weeks, then switch and choose another one to focus on for 1 to 2 weeks, repeat.

My 5 **POWER** quotes:

1.

2.

3.

4.

5.

Pha/e Four

By filling your mind with affirmations you are uploading data that you want your mind to believe. Affirmations are used to build your brain 'muscle'.

These **POWER Affirmations** I've chosen for you are from Chapter 19. Each morning you will say all 5 of them out loud with consistent, excited passion and desire! Pick 1 of the 5 affirmations to memorize and focus on specifically, for 1 to 2 weeks. Use it throughout each day as 'Maintenance' repeating it all day, when negative thoughts appear.

1. "Right now, I engage my mind, capture and replace my thoughts, and open the door for miracles, through belief and faith, with consistent practice, of my new wonderful mindset."
2. "Today, I choose to create a powerful mindset of grateful, thankful, forgiving, loving, appreciative, exciting, wonderful, inspirational, victorious thoughts because I will accept nothing short of an amazing, victorious, abundant life."
3. "I let go of the past and I choose today, to take command of my thoughts, and live in victory and abundance right now!"
4. "I choose right now to take action, and deliberately practice, a grateful, victorious, abundant thought life, mindset, and attitude!"
5. "I am victorious, I am special, God only made one of me, and has an incredible perfect will for my life, and I'm taking it today!"

At some point in the near future you may begin to write your own. Put new wonderful thoughts in your mind all day. Stretch your mind every day with extraordinary powerful affirmations.

PHASE FIVE

I started by going online to the website Youtube.com and searched "inspirational videos." As I found people who greatly inspired me, I would get their CDs or DVDs. These I would use at home, in the car, and elsewhere to instantaneously motivate me. Examples are listed below of my favorites.[17]

Listen to or watch a motivational, inspirational CD, DVD or a YouTube video for five minutes.

List:

1.

2.

3.

PHASE SIX

Read a motivational, inspirational book for at least 5 minutes. This book should be immediate-type inspiration, not a novel.

List the books that I will use:

1.

2.

3.

---

[17] Les Brown, Team Hoyt, Joyce Meyer, Joel Osteen, Paul Potts on BGT, Tony Robbins, Jim Rohn, Nick Vujicic, Zig Ziegler.

DAILY POWER
maintenance system

Throughout your day, use the following to power yourself up and maintain your Victorious Mindset. It's a quick way to reenergize yourself:

Phase 1- your grateful list

Phase 3- your quotes list

Phase 4- your affirmation list

The next chapter is about getting physical with your mind. It goes right alongside this chapter and they should be used together. So keep reading and then come back and work these two chapters together.

CHAPTER SEVENTEEN VIDEOS[18]

The links provided below, will bring you to a video visual summary of what you just read. It is a fun and quick demonstration, by me personally, to be used as a working tool and resource for your continued growth toward YOUR Victorious Mindset!

The Daily Power Start and Maintenance System, Part 1:

http://youtu.be/9s-6YpW9WzY

The Daily Power Start and Maintenance System, Part 2:

http://youtu.be/rj0Y8DpDtuA

---

[18] "The author could have these videos remastered, but wanted to remain true to the realism of this initial training system and therefore, included videos as is. Some have slippage, but are still understandable. In the future, a remastered version will be available for purchase."

CHAPTER SEVENTEEN PERSONAL NOTES SECTION "DAILY POWER START AND MAINTENANCE SYSTEM"

_____

_____

_____

_____

_____

_____

_____

_____

_____

_____

_____

_____

_____

_____

_____

_____

_____

_____

AUTHOR'S CHALLENGE

1. How often do you commit to applying, with passion, *"The Daily Power Start and Maintenance System?"*

Please Circle One:

1x per day

2x per day

3x per day

4x per day

All Day

CHAPTER EIGHTEEN

GET PHYSICAL WITH YOUR MIND

Surround yourself with victorious thoughts and victorious people and you will be victorious!

Chip Esajian, Motivational Coach

W hile completing the first four "Phases" of *The Victorious Mindset* "Daily Power Start and Maintenance System" in Chapter 17, you need to be somewhere you can move around, jump up and down, walking back and forth, do *power moves*, stretching, etc.! This is important for forcing blood throughout your brain and body, to get control of your thoughts, attitudes, and actions immediately. You wake up your mind and body on your terms.

Some of the ways you can create 'power moves' is by: throwing your arms out to your sides or up in the air, crouch down bending your knees bouncing up and down a little bit, repeatedly lifting your body up and forward onto the balls of your feet and back down again, lifting your shoulders up-and-down, open and close your hands into fists.

Imagine yourself at a sports event and your team just won! Throw your arms up in the air, your excited, celebrate! Every morning shock and awe your body and mind into victory with passion, practice, and explosive energy.

You want to assume control of your mind and body from the minute you wake up until the minute your head hits the pillow at night!

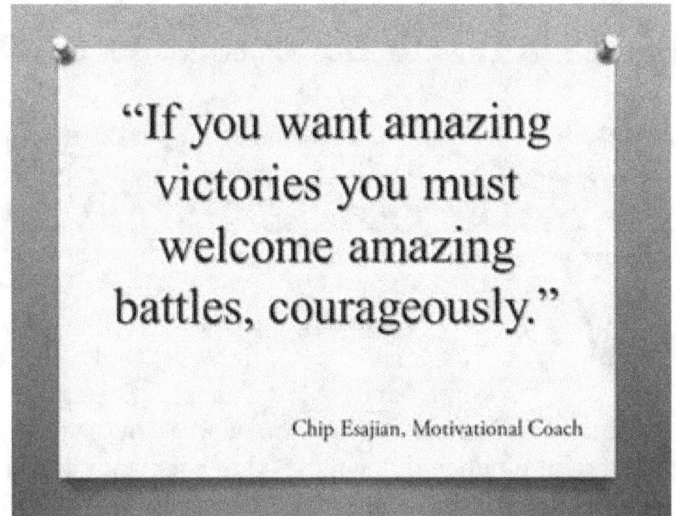

"If you want amazing victories you must welcome amazing battles, courageously."

Chip Esajian, Motivational Coach

CHAPTER EIGHTEEN PERSONAL NOTES SECTION "GET PHYSICAL WITH YOUR MIND"

_____

_____

_____

_____

_____

_____

_____

_____

_____

_____

_____

_____

_____

_____

_____

_____

_____

_____

AUTHOR'S CHALLENGE

Read and consider the questions listed below and fill in your answers. This helps provide a working tool and resource for your continued growth toward YOUR Victorious Mindset!

1. Within your daily schedule, where are a few places you can quickly go to and encourage yourself with your "Daily Power Maintenance System" victory routine?

   a. _____

   b. _____

   c. _____

2. What are your power moves?

   a. _____

   b. _____

   c. _____

CHAPTER NINETEEN

Victorious Battle Affirmations

Affirmation: The assertion that something exists or is true. Something that is affirmed; a statement or proposition that is declared to be true.

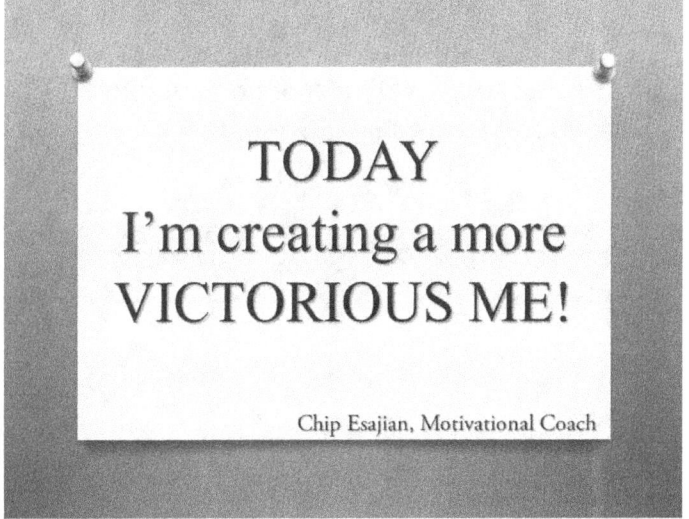

TODAY
I'm creating a more
VICTORIOUS ME!

Chip Esajian, Motivational Coach

By filling your mind with affirmations you are uploading data that you want your mind to believe, thus building your unlimited belief system!

You need to combine these affirmations with desire, passion, focus, and power moves!

Here is a list of a few of my "Victorious Battle Affirmations" I've put together that you can add in to your "Daily Power Start and Maintenance System."

Read these affirmations out loud with consistent, excited passion and desire!

"Today, right now, I choose
to create a powerful mindset of
grateful, thankful, forgiving, loving,
appreciative, exciting, wonderful,
inspirational, victorious thoughts
because I will accept nothing short
of an amazing,
victorious, abundant life."

Chip Esajian, Motivational Coach

"Right now, I choose to take responsibility for all that I have been blaming others for; I'm dumping the trash, on my way to an incredible, exciting, wonderful, abundant life that I've always imagined."

Chip Esajian, Motivational Coach

"Right now, I take full responsibility for every choice I have made in my entire life to this point, because I realize by taking responsibility, I am becoming a leader, and I have chosen to take control of my thoughts and create the life I've imagined! I am so excited about today's journey of the extraordinary life I have been given."

Chip Esajian, Motivational Coach

"Right now, I choose to forgive and let go of every negative thought for every person I am holding unforgiveness and negative thoughts against! Right now, I'm going for happiness in my life that gives me chills! It starts with forgiveness, gratefulness, hope, love and I'm going for extraordinary."

Chip Esajian, Motivational Coach

"Right now, I free my mind, drop the garbage, elevate my beliefs, run to the edge, leap, and fly towards my dreams."

Chip Esajian, Motivational Coach

"With courage, gratefulness and thankfulness, I engage my mindset for victory, believing the impossible is possible."

Chip Esajian, Motivational Coach

"Since perfect love casts out all fear, I choose today to take command of my thoughts, and live in victory and abundance right now!"

Chip Esajian, Motivational Coach

"I choose right now to take action, and deliberately practice a grateful, victorious, abundant thought life, mindset and attitude!"

Chip Esajian, Motivational Coach

"Right now, I'm practicing a wonderful thought life; I'm practicing grateful, thankful, exciting, loving, wonderful, giving, extraordinary, abundant thoughts that have nothing to do with the circumstances that I am floating above."

Chip Esajian, Motivational Coach

"Right now, today, I am becoming a grateful, thankful, happy, excited, and abundant new me that I am excited to be around! I'm happy, healthy, wealthy, excited, congruent, confident, and victorious! PBG is practicing, becoming, and giving in every area of my life."

Chip Esajian, Motivational Coach

"I am victorious in practicing, becoming, and now giving to others the victorious, abundance that I've created in my life, without thought of receiving but capturing the true fulfillment of pure giving."

Chip Esajian, Motivational Coach

"Today I'm courageous,
grateful and thankful I
engage my mindset and
believe the impossible to be
possible, and fly."

Chip Esajian, Motivational Coach

"Today, I dance with my fear
until it turns into courage,
because I will accept only
victory in my life knowing that
great victories require I
welcome great battles
courageously."

Chip Esajian, Motivational Coach

"I let go of the past and decide right now to live in victory, and take command of my thoughts and think wonderful, loving, giving, exciting, abundant thoughts."

Chip Esajian, Motivational Coach

"I am victorious, I am special, God only made one of me, and has an incredible perfect will for my life, and I'm taking it today!"

Chip Esajian, Motivational Coach

"Right now, I engage my mind, capture and replace my thoughts, open the door for miracles through belief and faith with continual practice of my new victorious mindset."

Chip Esajian, Motivational Coach

"Today, I begin my quest for extraordinary happiness by engaging and focusing my mindset on forgiveness; because I can go higher than I am. I was created for an amazing future."

Chip Esajian, Motivational Coach

"Today I'm passionate about freeing my mind and I forgive all my unforgiven. I forgive myself, friends, family and enemies. The greater purpose I am here for, I will not be deprived."

Chip Esajian, Motivational Coach

"I am a miracle created for the amazing purpose of creating a victorious mindset, to overflow extraordinary happiness, hope and love onto everyone I come in contact with."

Chip Esajian, Motivational Coach

"I'm successful, I'm creative, I'm imaginative, I'm loving, I'm giving, I'm supportive, I'm friendly and I'm grateful."

Chip Esajian, Motivational Coach

"Something wonderful is happening to me today!

My life is wonderful."

Chip Esajian, Motivational Coach

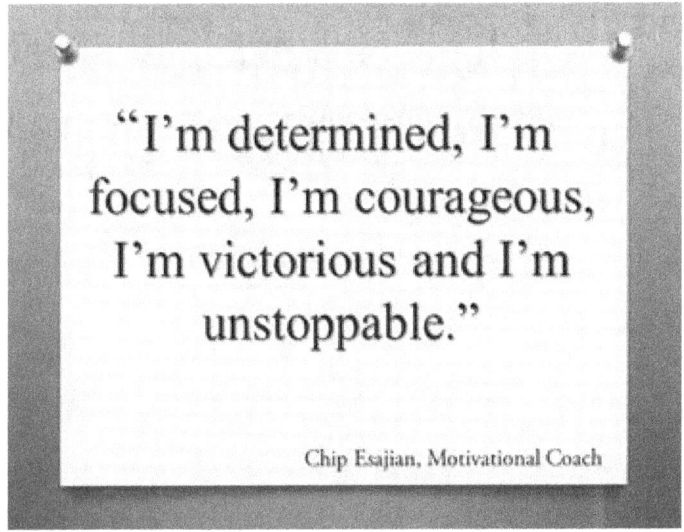

"I'm determined, I'm focused, I'm courageous, I'm victorious and I'm unstoppable."

Chip Esajian, Motivational Coach

These battle affirmations will get you started, as you can add to them and create your own for your victorious and powerful journey ahead!

Chapter Nineteen Personal Notes Section "Battle Affirmations."

AUTHOR'S CHALLENGE

In addition to the routine you have set up for yourself already in Chapter 17, "The Daily Power Start and Maintenance System," write out the following on individual cards or pieces of paper and post them in places where you will see them often throughout your day.

1. What are the three affirmations that you will commit to memorizing?

a. _____

b. _____

c. _____

CHAPTER TWENTY

Victorious Battle Quotes

Quote: To repeat (a passage, phrase, etc.) from a book, speech or the like, as by way of authority, illustration, etc.

Create a light at the
end of the tunnel,
even if you
don't see one!

Chip Esajian, Motivational Coach

Quotes of wisdom stretch our minds to think beyond our auto-pilot level of thinking!

Here are some quotes I have come up with along my own personal journey.

As my mind opened up from taking action daily and creating a Victorious Mindset, new inspirational quotes came to me!

It's a funny thing, when you stretch your mind, it expands and thinks bigger! Quotes will come to you also!

Remember what you focus on expands!

Here are quotes, which I'm sharing with you!

Make photo copies of the quotes that inspire and encourage you. Post them up around your home, in your car, and at your place of work!! Fill your life with encouragement and inspiration.

"Never give up
and create a better
you on the way to
your dreams."

Chip Esajian, Motivational Coach

"Become a contagious
virus of
EXTRAORDINARY
happiness and infect
everyone in your path."

Chip Esajian, Motivational Coach

"Power start your
morning with
gratefulness,
thankfulness, excitement,
then run to the edge,
jump, then fly."

Chip Esajian, Motivational Coach

"Step up to the edge,
believe, look up,
leap, and fly
towards your dreams."

Chip Esajian, Motivational Coach

"Be courageous, grateful, and thankful, engage your mindset for victory, and believe the impossible to be possible, and fly."

Chip Esajian, Motivational Coach

"Lean into and blow through your fears with courage, for only victory awaits you on the other side."

Chip Esajian, Motivational Coach

"Start looking at life with unlimited beliefs by believing all things are possible."

Chip Esajian, Motivational Coach

"What you focus on most you become, so engage your mind, and go for extraordinary abundance."

Chip Esajian, Motivational Coach

"Make no moment ordinary, for every moment is EXTRAORDINARY."

Chip Esajian, Motivational Coach

"Abundance, victory, and
happiness happen
by release of the past,
courage in the present, and
dreams of the future."

Chip Esajian, Motivational Coach

"Dance with your
fear until it turns
into courage."

Chip Esajian, Motivational Coach

"Empty the trash in
your mind and
experience the miracle
in this moment."

Chip Esajian, Motivational Coach

"An attitude of gratitude
will elevate your altitude,
so mount up with wings as
eagles and make it
a powerful day,
and be fearless!"

Chip Esajian, Motivational Coach

"Drop the weights, learn
to fly, and soar above
the mountains to see
your amazing purpose
before you."

Chip Esajian, Motivational Coach

"If you don't
work your mind,
your mind will work you,
so create
extraordinary abundance."

Chip Esajian, Motivational Coach

"An amazing attitude will create amazing results in your life! Create a big dream, then add passion, strategy, desire, discipline, powerful mindset, and accountability, and you will create an excitement in your life that is unstoppable!"

Chip Esajian, Motivational Coach

"You are special, you are gifted, you are amazing and you have the potential to accomplish anything, so make it a powerful day and be fearless!"

Chip Esajian, Motivational Coach

"Trying is an excuse to fail so
create a victorious mindset,
then CHOOSE
to do or not do!"

Chip Esajian, Motivational Coach

"Create a light at
the end of the
tunnel even if you
don't see one!"

Chip Esajian, Motivational Coach

"You're special, you're unique, you're beautiful, no one looks like you, you were created for EXTRAORDINARY!

⸙ Chip Esajian, Motivational Coach

"Our mental attitude determines our thoughts, our thoughts determine our altitude, our altitude determines our choices, our choices determine our path and our path determines our destination. Practice your dreams!"

Chip Esajian, Motivational Coach

"There is a solution to every real problem as long as you don't add imaginary problems to the equation."

Chip Esajian, Motivational Coach

"Practice inspiration, become inspiration, give inspiration!"

Chip Esajian, Motivational Coach

"Practice forgiveness,
become forgiveness,
give forgiveness!"

Chip Esajian, Motivational Coach

"Practice happiness,
become happiness,
give happiness!"

Chip Esajian, Motivational Coach

"Be an
EXTRAORDINARY
friend to others
by creating a life of
VICTORIOUS hope
others are inspired by."

Chip Esajian, Motivational Coach

"Get the 'can't's' and 'buts' out of your
vocabulary, then 'do' and 'be' the
extraordinary person you were
created to be."

Chip Esajian, Motivational Coach

"Abundance, victory, and happiness happen by release of the past, courage in the present, and dreams of the future."

Chip Esajian, Motivational Coach

"If you practice happiness all day long, how good can you get at it?"

Chip Esajian, Motivational Coach

"Inner peace begins with forgiveness!"

Chip Esajian, Motivational Coach

"Change is always happening, embrace it, be grateful for it and enjoy it!"

Chip Esajian, Motivational Coach

"Care about people, not what you want from them, but what you can give them and you will have all you want!"

Chip Esajian, Motivational Coach

"When you fall down, get up and infuse victorious happiness as your only destination for you are a miracle that someone is influenced by."

Chip Esajian, Motivational Coach

"Your only limits are in your mind, so blow through your fears and believe."

Chip Esajian, Motivational Coach

"Once you forgive you can truly begin to live!"

Chip Esajian, Motivational Coach

"It's never too late to
realize your dreams
since they have
no age limit!"

Chip Esajian, Motivational Coach

"Everything we do today
echoes into our future for
all we know;
so practice, become,
and give victory!"

Chip Esajian, Motivational Coach

"If you want a happiness in your life that gives you chills, then forgive, become grateful, become hopeful and give love!"

Chip Esajian, Motivational Coach

"Instead of just surviving today, mental shift into THRIVING!"

Chip Esajian, Motivational Coach

"You are only one
thought away from
a wonderful day!"

Chip Esajian, Motivational Coach

"Invest in yourself, practice
liking you, for the greatest
high in life is giving hope
and encouragement to
another life."

Chip Esajian, Motivational Coach

"Life is incredible,
by the altitude of
thoughts we choose
to create!"

Chip Esajian, Motivational Coach

"Strive to thrive and
not just to survive,
and become alive!"

Chip Esajian, Motivational Coach

"To have a better future, stop looking in the past, focus on the present, and enjoy the day, for it is the present; what a gift!"

Chip Esajian, Motivational Coach

"If you fail, keep moving forward because success is right around the corner."

Chip Esajian, Motivational Coach

"If you don't get out
of your comfort zone,
you will never go
where you wish you
were."

Chip Esajian, Motivational Coach

"Create the change
you want to happen in
your life!"

Chip Esajian, Motivational Coach

"Dream out of your reach, get your mind set, believe the impossible is possible, focus, do extraordinary, and leap."

Chip Esajian, Motivational Coach

"Give more and expect less, and set yourself up for success."

Chip Esajian, Motivational Coach

"Be grateful, be interested in people, be optimistic, give value, have fun, lighten up, let go of the past, and laugh."

Chip Esajian, Motivational Coach

"There are two ways to look younger; first is let go of the past, lighten up, have fun, smile and laugh, or 2nd shave your head."

Chip Esajian, Motivational Coach

"Stepping from ordinary into extraordinary, requires letting go of your past, so you can focus on the path."

Chip Esajian, Motivational Coach

"What you focus on expands, and that you become, so focus on happiness."

Chip Esajian, Motivational Coach

"To engage this Extraordinary moment, disengage from the moments before and dispose of the moments that are to come!"

Chip Esajian, Motivational Coach

"We judge others by the image we have of ourselves, so create a wonderful self-image and watch loving replace judging."

Chip Esajian, Motivational Coach

"Do you brighten a room by entering or exiting it? Create a mindset of power, victory, and abundance."

Chip Esajian, Motivational Coach

"Belief, faith and hope will emerge, when forgiveness is recognized!"

Chip Esajian, Motivational Coach

"We have such an incredible opportunity to live the life of our dreams right in our mind!"

Chip Esajian, Motivational Coach

"Engage your mind, focus your thoughts and believe all things are possible."

Chip Esajian, Motivational Coach

"The fear, anxiety and bitterness you have about any person or situation, you have created; delete it."

Chip Esajian, Motivational Coach

"Our attitude is determined by the negative thoughts that run our lives or by the wonderful thoughts we choose to create."

Chip Esajian, Motivational Coach

"When negative thoughts come; capture and replace them with wonderful abundant thoughts."

Chip Esajian, Motivational Coach

"Go for your dreams, develop a powerful mindset of abundance, make a plan, and dare to be courageous."

Chip Esajian, Motivational Coach

"To be a servant and
to bless people's lives
is the highest calling."

Chip Esajian, Motivational Coach

"Realizing your true
vulnerability is power beyond
all measure, for it causes
EXTRAORDINARY gratitude
for the miracle you are and the
gift you've been given."

Chip Esajian, Motivational Coach

"What could you accomplish if fear was removed from your thought process? Remove it and fly."

Chip Esajian, Motivational Coach

"Fear is an illusion, so delete it from your mindset."

Chip Esajian, Motivational Coach

"A Dream is just a
dream until you
create the mindset to
take the first step."

Chip Esajian, Motivational Coach

"Only YOU hold you
back, so let go, break
the chains and engage
an extraordinary
abundant life."

Chip Esajian, Motivational Coach

"If your thought life discourages you, then choose to take action towards victorious abundance."

Chip Esajian, Motivational Coach

"Problems are a sign that you're alive, so turn them into opportunities."

Chip Esajian, Motivational Coach

"Take the time to create a victorious thought life that gives you constant excitement."

Chip Esajian, Motivational Coach

"You're here on planet earth, so why not choose a powerful victorious life built on gratefulness and thankfulness."

Chip Esajian, Motivational Coach

"Create extraordinary happiness from extreme gratefulness, not from financial or circumstantial gain or loss, and build a bridge above anxiety and fear."

Chip Esajian, Motivational Coach

"Daily you stop at red lights, knowing they turn green, so live the same for your dreams."

Chip Esajian, Motivational Coach

"Forget the past, forgive your un-forgiven, possess the present, and dream a big dream."

Chip Esajian, Motivational Coach

"Get addicted to thinking wonderful, uplifting, encouraging thoughts every moment of every day, and watch the fear, and doubt fall away."

Chip Esajian, Motivational Coach

"Every life you give a breath of victory and hope to, adds to the extraordinary abundance in your own life."

Chip Esajian, Motivational Coach

"To encourage another towards victory in their life is to create another level of happiness and abundance in yours."

Chip Esajian, Motivational Coach

"Take every opportunity today to live in victory through gratefulness, thankfulness, and looking for the best in others."

Chip Esajian, Motivational Coach

"Where you are tomorrow starts today and since you're not promised tomorrow, this moment is at hand."

Chip Esajian, Motivational Coach

"Overcome your fear with incredible courage through building a powerful mindset of victory"

Chip Esajian, Motivational Coach

"Lean into and blow through your fears with courage, for only victory awaits you on the other side."

Chip Esajian, Motivational Coach

"Fear is false evidence appearing real, so engage your mind, and blow through your fears with courage."

Chip Esajian, Motivational Coach

"Believe beyond what you see and achieve extraordinary in your life."

Chip Esajian, Motivational Coach

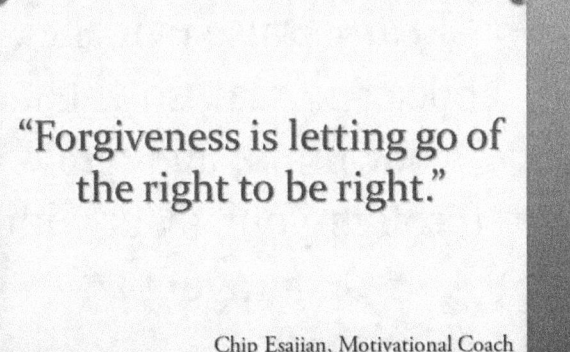

"Forgiveness is letting go of the right to be right."

Chip Esajian, Motivational Coach

"Make every day Saturday, turn work into play and create an extraordinary day."

Chip Esajian, Motivational Coach

"Create an extraordinary relationship with yourself and add extreme value to everyone you come in contact with."

Chip Esajian, Motivational Coach

"Your relationship with yourself affects everyone around you, so are you enjoying you or ready to get a divorce?"

Chip Esajian, Motivational Coach

"Stop waiting for something wonderful to happen to you! Instead take charge of your mind and create an extraordinary grateful life that will inspire others."

Chip Esajian, Motivational Coach

"All results are victorious and successful if you use them to propel you towards happiness."

Chip Esajian, Motivational Coach

"Your defeats were
followed by victories
for here you stand, so
be victorious."

Chip Esajian, Motivational Coach

"If you want a more
exciting life, create a
more amazing you."

Chip Esajian, Motivational Coach

"Having a dream is a thought, engaging your goals is the journey and creating a victorious mindset is for the day at hand;
for happiness is success."

Chip Esajian, Motivational Coach

"You're special, wonderful and amazing! There's no one with your fingerprint, so make this day more than ordinary!"

Chip Esajian, Motivational Coach

"Stuffing the trash in your mind holds you back from your extraordinary purpose, so let it go and watch life flow."

Chip Esajian, Motivational Coach

"Get an extraordinary courageous mindset, use the storms of life to propel you towards your dreams and never ever give up."

Chip Esajian, Motivational Coach

"Instead of worrying about financial gain or loss, create a victorious life that takes your own breath away."

Chip Esajian, Motivational Coach

"Create an unlimited victorious mindset, engage wonderful habits, surround yourself with happy people and success will be yours."

Chip Esajian, Motivational Coach

"Make Extraordinary your only destination. See it, make the choice, take action now and BELIEVE."

Chip Esajian, Motivational Coach

"To live extreme victory is to go for Extraordinary, miss and still hit wonderful."

Chip Esajian, Motivational Coach

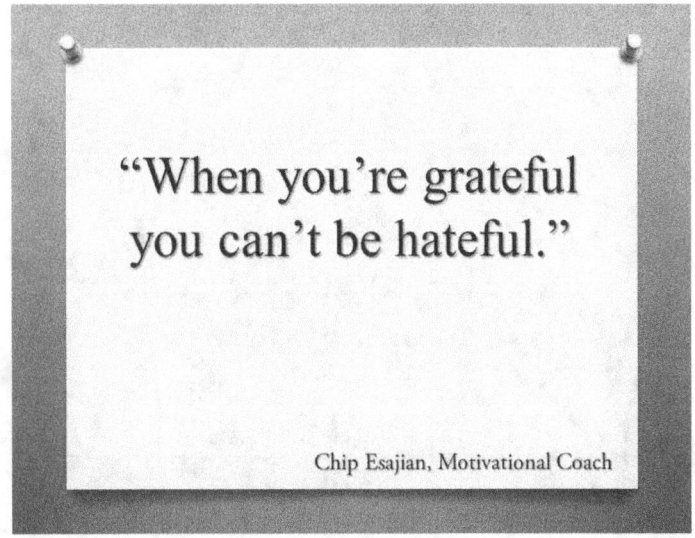

"When you're grateful you can't be hateful."

Chip Esajian, Motivational Coach

These quotes will push your mind to expand to new possibilities for your life!

You can carry 3x5 cards with you everywhere you go by writing these affirmations and quotes on them for easy review.

You can look for and purchase, "The Victorious Mindset Affirmation Cards" and associated mobile apps too!

Just make certain you use the affirmation cards daily.

Remember, how much you practice your new Victorious Mindset techniques is how fast your results will come!

Chapter Twenty Personal Notes Section For "Victorious Battle Quotes"

_____

_____

_____

_____

_____

_____

_____

_____

_____

_____

_____

_____

_____

_____

_____

_____

_____

_____

_____

_____

_____

_____

AUTHOR'S CHALLENGE

I found, by looking at quotes, saying them, repeating them, and memorizing them - I was able to make room in my mind for possibilities in life I had never thought of before. It's time for you to battle for bigger in your mind.

1. What are your top 5 favorite "Victorious Battle Quotes"?

a. _____

b. _____

c. _____

d. _____

e. _____

2. Why do these 5 quotes inspire you?

a. _____

b. _____

c. _____

d. _____

e. _____

CHAPTER TWENTY-ONE

NEW MINDSET
NEW FRIENDS

Mindset: An attitude, disposition or mood.

Friend: A person attached to another by feelings of affection or personal regard.

Change is always happening, embrace it, be grateful for it and enjoy it!

Chip Esajian, Motivational Coach

A brand new world is opening up before your eyes; and your mountains are moving out of the path of your dreams, that you are now beginning to see. There is another step in the system, which is very important to the continued growth of your new Victorious Mindset. You now should be looking at your friends very differently.

Because you have eliminated scarcity from your life, it will become very apparent very quickly who your friends are and if they are coming from a place of scarcity or abundance.

> "When you raise your standards of who you are, you clearly see who you were and can embrace who you want to become."
>
> Chip Esajian, Motivational Coach

Who you hang out with is who you are. With that in mind, you now need to get very picky about the people you spend your time with.

If you want to continue to elevate your altitude with a victorious attitude, then those are the kind of people you need to be surrounding yourself with. If you spend your time with people that complain, whine, moan, talk bad about other people, judge, and procrastinate, etc. guess what? That is who you become!

If you spend your time with people that are victorious, happy, excited, grateful, thankful, abundant, have huge dreams and goals, who love life, etc. guess what? That is who you become. THERE IS NO IN BETWEEN

HELLO!!!!! YOU ARE EITHER ONE OR THE OTHER.

If you are saying; *"But Chip my friends need me!"* Great, invite them to come spend time with you and your new friends in your new environment, and set firm boundaries for yourself, so you continue to fly toward your dreams.

Remember, YOU control how fast the doors to your dreams are unlocked. How focused you are on your mission to free your mind and life, is how fast the mountains can be moved out of your way on your journey to your dreams! How strong is your new faith you have developed?

Choose your friends wisely.

CHapter Twenty-one Videos[19]

The links provided below, will bring you to a video visual summary of what you just read. It is a fun and quick demonstration, by me personally, to be used as a working tool and resource for your continued growth toward YOUR Victorious Mindset!

New Mindset /New Friends Part1:
http://youtu.be/pFc5sG_prO0

New Mindset /New Friends Part2:
http://youtu.be/C3dv_wGoxuA

New Mindset /New Friends Part 3:
http://youtu.be/yhS1fiWkIiU

---

19 "The author could have these videos remastered, but wanted to remain true to the realism of this initial training system and therefore, included videos as is. Some have slippage, but are still understandable. In the future, a remastered version will be available for purchase."

CHAPTER TWENTY-ONE
PERSONAL NOTES SECTION FOR "NEW MINDSET, NEW FRIENDS"

_____

_____

_____

_____

_____

_____

_____

_____

_____

_____

_____

_____

_____

_____

_____

_____

_____

_____

_____

_____

AUTHOR'S CHALLENGE

It's important for you to think about these two questions carefully, to be honest with yourself, and commit to putting it in writing.

1. What are the top 5 qualities you want and expect in a friend?

a. _____

b. _____

c. _____

d. _____

e. _____

2. What are the top 5 qualities you bring to your friendships?

a. _____

b. _____

c. _____

d. _____

e. _____

CHAPTER TWENTY-TWO

YOU NEED COACHES, ACCOUNTABILITY AND DISCIPLINE IN LIFE

Coaches: To give instruction or advice to in the capacity of a coach; instruct.

Accountability: The state of being accountable, liable, or answerable.

Discipline: exercise, or a regimen that develops or improves a skill; training.

> You're here on planet earth, so why not choose a powerful victorious life built on gratefulness and thankfulness!
>
> Chip Esajian, Motivational Coach

In life I've learned we need coaches. We need people to help us with accountability, discipline, goals, passion, and desire to achieve our dreams and goals. We need people around us to support the road we're on. It's easy to lose focus on the journey. How many times have you started a project, task, or goal only to not complete it?

As you elevate your mindset, you will elevate your opportunities in life. As your opportunities in life open up you will be stepping into unknown territories that you will need guidance and direction in. That is why it is so very important to have people in your life to keep you accountable to achieving your dreams and goals whatever they may be.

As I changed my mindset; my inward life, views, beliefs, and dreams changed. I have coaches in life that I've made myself accountable to for my continued growth. Why? Because we, by ourselves, cannot see higher than we know, but when we surround ourselves with people that have been and are where we want to be, we can get there quicker making fewer mistakes with guides. Learn from others' mistakes instead of your own and you will get to your destination quicker.

For example, if you want to go on a jungle safari, you hire a jungle safari guide. Why? Because he knows his way through the jungle, and has been there many times before; he can show you the shortcuts and safe paths, while helping you to avoid the dangers to stay away from. You won't have to make the same mistakes that you would have if you just wandered into that same jungle without a guide. Can you image? You've got to stay on course.

Why waste precious time going around in circles when you can have coaches in your life to help get you there faster! I have a few different coaches in my life for different purposes, and all of them have coaches that push them to achieve higher levels of extraordinary! Why you may ask? Because we are not truly happy in life unless we are pushing forward in life, pushing past old limitations to build new unlimited beliefs! You have amazing potential inside of you, and you were created for extraordinary, whatever that looks like to you. Whether that is just being the best teacher, librarian, mechanic, salesman, etc. Remember, this journey is about building an inner wealth you've never had, to live an extraordinary life of happiness and abundance that you've never experienced before. Everyone wants purpose. That is what everyone dreams of.

Let me ask you a question. Once you learn how to create extraordinary happiness, do you think it stops there? Do you think you've arrived? My friends, the journey has just begun and your levels of growth will never end.

You can and will create amazing results in a short time. Then when your life begins to change you will want more happiness, higher levels of gratefulness, thankfulness, excitement, giving, and amazing abundance!

Our mind is like a water glass. If you fill up a glass with water and leave it sitting on a table for 1 month without drinking it or pouring it out, what happens to that water? What will it look like? What will it smell like? What will it taste like? It will begin to change color, it will begin to smell bad, and it will taste bad! It is the same with our minds. Now what if you leave that same glass of 1 month old water there for 6 months, 1 year, or 2 years? Have you ever been to a swamp?

How are we any different if we are not consistently refilling ourselves? For an exciting, wonderful, fulfilled abundant life, we have to continue to fill up on wonderful thoughts to pour out and over flow onto others. That means we have to continually fill up our glass to continue to pour out sparkling clear water. If you keep giving amazing value to others you will have room to keep filling up your cup. We have to continue to stay in "shape" if you will! If you stop using a muscle in your body, what happens? It forgets how to perform. It gets out of shape because it's not being used.

If you golfed every day for 10 years then stopped playing for 2 years, how good do you think you would play that first time out on the course? What would your game look like after 2 years of not picking up a golf club? Slice here, slice there, right? You would get really frustrated. Not only that, but how would you feel emotionally after not playing for 2 years, then you go out and play terrible? You would have a miserable time. You set yourself up to fail instead of succeed. That is going to be the longest 18 holes you ever played!

What happened? You simply stopped using those specific muscles on a daily basis; which caused you to get out of shape. The result is your inability to perform at the level you used to when you practiced consistently.

My point is that if we're not moving forward we're moving backward. You are either building victorious abundance or slipping back into scarcity. You are either learning, practicing, becoming, and giving or you are going in the opposite direction.

This book is simple, but applying the content of this book in your life 24 hours a day, for the rest of your life is going to take serious focus, accountability, coaching, discipline, time management, mind management, goals, and dreams. To do that, you need people in your life that will not let you slack off. You need to be around people that will push you forward towards a more victorious life with momentum right alongside of them.

Go for extraordinary and do whatever it takes to stay on track; and make sure you have the destination already plugged into MapQuest so your directions will be laid out for you!

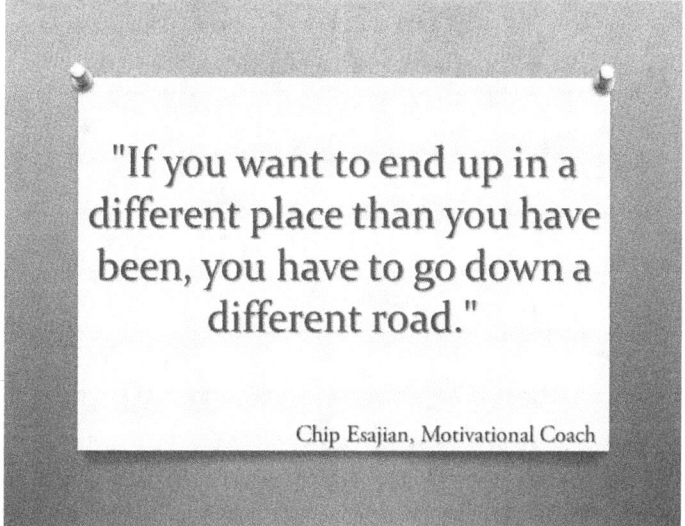

"If you want to end up in a different place than you have been, you have to go down a different road."

Chip Esajian, Motivational Coach

Chapter Twenty-Two
Personal Notes Section
"Coaches, Accountability and Discipline"

_____

_____

_____

_____

_____

_____

_____

_____

_____

_____

_____

_____

_____

_____

_____

_____

_____

AUTHOR'S CHALLENGE

Read and consider the questions listed below and fill in your answers. This helps provide a working tool and resource for your continued growth toward YOUR Victorious Mindset!

1. Who is coaching you? (this can be someone's books, videos, and audios you follow as well as someone in person who coaches you)

   a.

   b.

   c.

2. Who are you accountable to?

   a.

   b.

   c.

3. What new disciplines are you establishing in your life right now?

   a.

   b.

   c.

CHAPTER TWENTY-THREE

Congratulations

> Engage your mind, focus your thoughts and believe all things are possible!
>
> Chip Esajian, Motivational Coach

You now have "The Victorious Mindset Training System" to develop the mindset necessary to build the bridge to your dreams and goals.

Keep it simple! Focus, engage, and practice with passion! You now know what you have to do. This is a life journey and you can have extraordinary rewards in a short time! Make it your dream to have incredible happiness to give to others. When you're overflowing with wonderful, it will spill onto everyone you come in contact with. Your greatest joy will be seeing others being hungry for what you have, and you being able to give them treasure greater than money!

Read this power book over and over again! Study it, and burn it into your mind as you practice and put your mind into high gear power training for ultimate results!

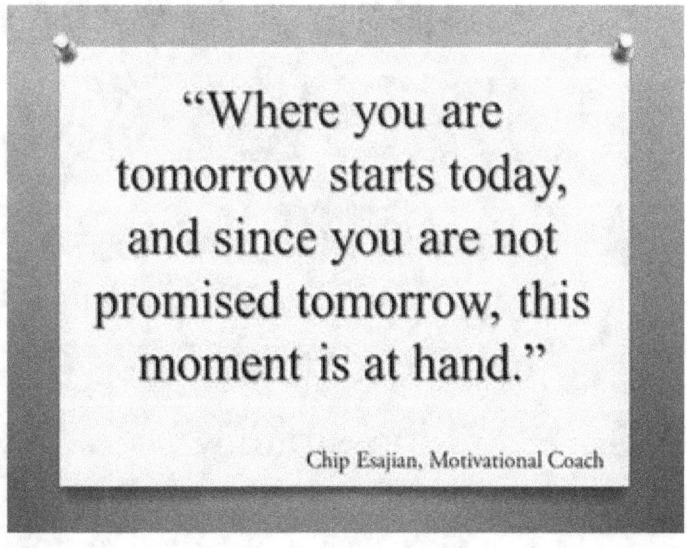

"Where you are tomorrow starts today, and since you are not promised tomorrow, this moment is at hand."

Chip Esajian, Motivational Coach

You have embarked on an incredible journey like no other you have ever encountered nor knew existed! You now have the tools! What you do with them is your "choice." The life you "choose" to live is up to you.

I am so humbly grateful for the honor given me to share *The Victorious Mindset* with you!

Choose to live an amazing victorious life to create such value that others will want what you have!

> "Create extraordinary happiness from extreme gratefulness, not from financial or circumstantial gain or loss, and build an amazing bridge above anxiety and fear."
>
> Chip Esajian, Motivational Coach

Remember live light, have a sense of humor, be able to laugh at yourself, and let go of having to be right. Practice, become, give, dream, and live for others and focus on such a big dream that you have to have God's help to achieve it! Happiness is success and it's an extraordinary journey!

Be victorious and courageous in all you do!

"As a man thinks in his heart, so is he . . . " [20]

"Go for EXTRAORDINARY, for there is only ONE YOU."

---

[20] Prov. 23:7

BATTLE NOTES

BATTLE NOTES

BATTLE NOTES

BATTLE NOTES

BATTLE NOTES

BATTLE NOTES

BATTLE NOTES

BATTLE NOTES

BATTLE NOTES

BATTLE NOTES

BATTLE NOTES

BATTLE NOTES

Index

U

V

W

Y

Z

ABOUT THE AUTHOR

CHIP ESAJIAN

C hip Esajian is an ordinary person who has lived an extraordinary life. He's been a Chippendale's dancer, actor, ministry home overseer, car detailer, real estate agent, and mortgage banker; fueled by his gift of "encouragement," he wants to show you how to see the mountains move out of the way of your dreams.

Chip is a happily married man with 3 wonderful children, who currently resides in California, in the United States of America.

VISIT CHIP ESAJIAN

SOCIAL MEDIA

FACEBOOK
https://www.facebook.com/AuthorChipEsajian#

https://www.facebook.com/chipesajianfanpage

TWITTER
https://twitter.com/VictoriousNook

http://www.twitter.com/chipesajian

YOUTUBE:
http://www.youtube.com/user/DonnaInk

http://www.youtube.com/chipesajian

BLOGS

WORDPRESS
http://authorchipesajian.wordpress.com

TO PURCHASE

DonnaInk Publications: www.donnaink.org

AUTHOR WEBSITES

www.chipesajian.com

www.chipesajianbook.com

DonnaInk Publications, L.L.C.
www . d o n n a i n k . o r g

Publisher
www.donnaink.org

For more information:
bulk orders and/or marketing and promotions
contact the Special Markets Division of
DonnaInk Publications, L.L.C.
at special_markets@donnaink.org.

ZENCON ART OF
ZEN CONSULTANCY

PR & Marketing
www.zenconartofzen.com

www.ingramcontent.com/pod-product-compliance
Lightning Source LLC
Chambersburg PA
CBHW070835280626
47161CB00015B/655